Christmas Can Be Murder
A Morton novella

Sean Campbell

Christmas Can Be Murder

First published in Great Britain by De Minimis 2019

© Sean Campbell 2019

The moral rights of Sean Campbell to be identified as the author of this work has been asserted by them in accordance with the Copyright, Designs and Patents Act 1988.

Cover Art designed by MiblArt

All characters are fictitious. Any resemblance to real persons, living or dead, is purely coincidental.

First Edition

Chapter 1: Crofte's Department Store

The message came in during the dead of night.

For DCI David Morton, being paged came with the territory: every one of London's twenty-eight Murder Investigation Teams had to suffer being on call at ungodly hours and his was no exception.

But the number on the phone didn't belong to the Met switchboard. Instead it was marked "Leon Yap". There was a blast from the past. The message read:

I need to call in that favour. Come to Crofte's. Right now.

Against his better judgement Morton rolled out of bed and got dressed. He then grabbed his go-bag, kissed Sarah gently on the forehead so as not to wake her, and headed out into the cold of Christmas Eve. The roads were deserted and he arrived in next to no time and found a parking spot within sight of the legendary department store. Morton emerged onto the pavement cursing the weather as his foot struggled to gain purchase on the ice. Behind him, the roundel sign for Sloane Square hung from the entrance to the tube station while ahead of him was Crofte's Department Store, its enormous arch-shaped window filled with a Christmas tree large enough to rival the one in Trafalgar Square. As he plodded gingerly towards the store, the tree's lights worked their way through a pattern of red, blue, green and purple, the twinkling lights and absolute silence giving the morning a surreal vibe. It was four thirty in the morning, bang in the middle of what Morton called the twilight hours, the time when the area, which in a few hours' time would be bustling with tourists, became unnaturally still. The bars had been shut for hours, the last lingering drunks chased from the streets by the snow, and the many upmarket shops of the Kings Road were not due to open for hours.

As Morton reached the main entrance, the revolving door sprang to life and the man that Morton had com to meet waved at him from the other side of the glass. Moments later Morton crossed the threshold, a welcome column of warm air greeting him.

'David!' Leon said. 'Sorry to wake you.'

At first blush Leon looked exactly as Morton remembered him: lean to the point of being skinny with slicked-back hair worthy of a used cars salesman. These days his full-sleeve tattoos were hidden beneath a thread-worn shirt that was bulging around the middle. Ruddy cheeks and ashen skin etched with wrinkles undermined Leon's formerly youthful charm. He was jumpier, less sure of himself, and he was sweating profusely as if he'd run a mile.

Morton eyed him warily. 'You didn't give me much choice, now, did you, Leon?'

'You owe me one,' Leon said.

'I *did* owe you one,' Morton corrected him. 'Twenty years ago. It's a bit late to be calling in that favour now.'

Another smile, this one sadder than the last. 'Yet here you are, loyal to the last. I guess I'd best tell you why I woke you at four am. Before I do....'

His voice trailed off and then he bit his lip nervously as if afraid of how Morton would react to what he was about to say.

'Out with it, for Pete's sake. I've got my Christmas shopping to do in a few hours,' Morton said.

'You know I'm not crazy right?' Leon said. 'I know some of you lot think I am, see. What I'm about to tell you, well, you might think so too. It's going to sound ludicrous and if I'm right about something, it's going to get *weird*. I need to know you still trust me.'

As he spoke, Leon led Morton through the maze of beauty concessions and the centre of the store.

It had been forever since he'd seen him and yet as Morton fell into lockstep beside him, it felt natural. Like so many of Morton's adult friendships, they'd just drifted apart when their lives took them in different directions and Leon's life had careened off a cliff pretty quickly. There were always rumours about undercover detectives and Leon had sent the rumour mill running wild. He'd been deep undercover working for the Bakowski Crime Syndicate when one of the big newspapers, *The Impartial*, had plastered his face on the front cover and outed him as a dirty cop. The Bakowski brothers hadn't taken too kindly to learning that their right-hand man was an undercover detective.

'Leon, what happened to you wasn't your fault.'

The security guard shifted uncomfortably, his hands thrust deep in his pockets.

'I know, I know. I'm not perfect though. You know I used to like a drink or two?'

'We both did back then,' Morton said. 'Though I stopped that pretty sharpish.'

Their last drinking session had been the Christmas before Leon was fired. Several pints past merry, Morton had suggested going carolling. He'd butchered *Fairytale of New York* – Sarah's favourite song – so badly that a passer-by offered to pay him to shut up. Ever since the Great Christmas Carol Extortion had become a family tradition.

'I didn't,' Leon said flatly. 'And last night...'

'You had a few.'

'I may have had a festive tipple. But that doesn't mess up what I saw, David. I swear it doesn't.'

'What did you see?'

Leon stopped abruptly and stared down at his feet, acutely aware that he was about to be mocked mercilessly. 'Santa Claus,' he half-whispered.

Morton rolled his eyes. 'And Rudolph the reindeer too? You don't seriously believe in that Santa malarkey, do you?'

'Not since Santa stopped visiting me when I moved out of my parents' house thirty years ago.'

'Did you forget to fill out the change of address form?' Morton scoffed. The lift door pinged again to signal that they'd reached the top floor.

'I don't think it *was* Santa Claus. Just someone dressed up as him. Look, I'll prove it to you.'

As the pair emerged into the centre of the store, its full glory of the store came into view. Now Morton could look up and see all the floors above him arranged in a bull ring and beyond them the stained-glass windows of the roof.

'There,' Leon said. He pointed at the huge Christmas tree that Morton had seen as he'd approached the store. It looked as if it reached up to the roof six floors above and so Morton reckoned it had to be at least sixty-foot-high. It was bedecked in what looked like thousands of fairy lights and an equal number of ornaments in all shapes and sizes. Underneath it were dozens of ornately-wrapped boxes.

'So?'

'See those six presents that jut out on the end, the ones that make the display look asymmetrical? Those weren't there last night. And that little one on the end is oozing blood.'

He had lost it. From where Morton was standing, the display looked like it did every year: over the top, elegant, and an obvious tourist magnet.

'Leon,' Morton said gently, 'are you sure? How much did you drink last night? Are you still drunk?'

'No, I'm bloody not. I know it sounds insane but I know what I saw.' Leon said. 'I've been working this store day and night for nearly a decade. You think I don't know the Christmas display that I've walked past a dozen times a day every day since mid-November?'

He wrung his hands as he spoke, a slight jitter attracting Morton's attention. Leon was on edge in a way that Morton had never seen before.

'Okay,' Morton said. 'Let's pretend for a moment that I believe you, that those presents magically appeared this morning. What do you want me to do about it? Charge Santa with reverse shop-lifting?'

As they approached the tree, Leon glared. 'David, look again, more closely – I'm talking about the three red boxes on the left besides that giant Teddy Bear. See the blood leaking out of that one in the middle?'

He was right. A tiny pool of blood was seeping out from underneath the smallest parcel. It wasn't much to look at and Morton was astonished at how perceptive his friend must have been to have spotted it.

Morton stopped in his tracks. 'We've got to call in the Scene of Crime Officers.'

'On Crimble?' Leon said, his tone suggesting that he knew it wasn't going to happen. 'Forget that. David, do me a favour and stay where you are. You're too far away to stop me, right? But close enough to see the box is untouched, that I haven't fiddled with it before now?'

Morton hesitated. It was a big ask and it was the reason Leon hadn't opened the box when he'd first found it: he wanted Morton to witness Leon opening the box so that it wouldn't be incriminating if his fingerprints were on it. He did owe Leon. But why did Leon know to contact him if he hadn't seen what was inside? Was it just an abundance of caution over the false rumours that had got him in trouble before? Before Morton could protest, Leon made the decision for him: he leapt past him and began to tug at the ends of the silk bow which adorned the top of the present. It came undone in one easy movement freeing the lid. As Morton watched, Leon gingerly lifted it.

Straight away, the sides of the box fell down.

There, in the middle of the box, finger pointed upwards in a rude gesture, was what appeared to be a human hand sitting in a pool of blood.

A wail escaped Leon's lips, desperate and uncontrollable. He sank to his knees, sobbing s in fits. Morton knelt down next to him, being careful not to come into contact with the blood slick on the floor.

As Morton stepped closer, he could see that the ridges he had taken for wrinkles were, in fact, sculpted out of wax. Whoever had made it had taken the time to paint the fingernails such that they were adorned with tiny Christmas trees flecked with snow. There was even a ring on one finger.

'It's not real, Leon,' Morton said. 'Breathe. It's just a prank. It's wax and that's not real blood.'

Raspy breaths escaped Leon as he struggled to bring himself under control, 'The... the... the ring...'

Morton followed his gaze. The ring was tiny, a diamond no larger than a speck on a simple gold band that was tarnished with age.

'It's Kaylee's,' Leon said. His voice stronger, more certain. 'It's my Kaylee's wedding ring.'

Without skipping a beat, Morton reached into his jacket pocket for his mobile. 'I'm calling it in.'

As he dialled, Leon rose and placed a hand on his wrist. 'Don't!'

His heart sank as he cast a troubled gaze at Leon. There was only one good reason not to call it in. He had to ask anyway. 'Why shouldn't I call it in, Leon?'

There was a moment's hesitation before Leon broke.

'Because I'm in trouble, David. Big trouble.'

'You know who did this.' It wasn't a question.

'Tiny,' Leon said. 'Tiny Bakowski.'

Chapter 2: Confession

Morton's finger continued to hover above the call button.

'Start talking. Now.'

Leon hung his head. 'I... can't.'

The distance between finger and phone closed a little further. 'Last chance.'

'Please, David,' Leon said. 'You don't understand. They'll kill me.'

'I'll do it for them if you don't start talking. You asked me to come here for a reason. Your choice is pretty simple. I call in back-up, the Anti-Kidnap and Extortion Unit can deal with Kaylee's case, and I can go back to my merry little Christmas. Or you tell me what the hell is going on so I can try and help. As long as you haven't hurt anyone, I'm on your side.'

He shook his head slowly. 'Not here.'

With a click Morton locked his phone and then motioned for Leon to lead on.

Leon's eyes darted up to the ceiling where the eye-in-the-sky CCTV cameras watched everything below. He led Morton towards one side of the shop floor where, about fifty metres past the Christmas tree, Morton could see a door marked "staff only". When they reached it, Leon's belt jangled as he fiddled with the ring of keys on his belt until he found the key that would allow them access.

Once they were inside, the steel door shut behind them with a clang and Morton felt the telltale goosebumps on the back of his neck that often precipitated danger. Leon led him further in until, past another locked door, they found themselves in a bunker-like room with screens adorning three walls. Each showed one of the store's live CCTV feeds. Leon plonked himself down in the room's sole chair and swivelled to face Morton.

'I wouldn't,' Leon rasped. 'I mean I haven't. Hurt anyone that is.'

'Then talk. How'd you get caught up with Tiny Bakowski again?'

'Again?' Leon parroted. 'The Syndicate never let go the last time.'

Morton's mind flashed back to the old rumours that had circulated around the Met. Like most undercover officers, Leon's work was ill understood so when Leon had protested that it was all idle gossip, Morton had simply accepted his explanation and moved own. He knew from his own time undercover that it was easy for murmurs and speculation to spread and so he took it as red that the rumours about Leon were as unfounded as those circulating about Morton himself.

He sighed, his disappointment rising to the fore. 'Jesus, Leon. You really were dirty?'

Perhaps Leon wasn't the man he remembered after all. Perhaps he never had been.

'No,' Leon said. 'I wasn't. But I did things I wasn't proud of. I had no choice. There is no choice when you're dealing with a brute like Tiny.'

'There's always a choice, Leon. Always. What did he have on you and what did he ask of you? We're up against the clock so don't hold anything back.'

'You promise you won't arrest me?'

'I'm going to arrest you, Leon. The question is what for and how much I can tell the courts that you've cooperated.'

'I was forced to do it!'

'Then your barrister can raise duress as a defence in court,' Morton said. 'Your choice isn't "remain silent or be arrested" here. If you've broken the law, you'll be treated fairly like everyone else. The question is if we can save Kaylee's life first.'

His jaw set as he looked at Morton.

'Don't get angry with me, Leon,' Morton said. 'You brought me into this. Do you want my help or not?'

Quiet fell. The only sound Morton could hear was a tinny rendition of White Christmas coming from somewhere in the store.

'They threatened to kill her,' Leon finally said. 'Tiny and his brother that is. The same threat, over and over again. Do what we say or Kaylee dies. I should've known better but little by little, things from my real life crept into my gang persona. I know that's not how it's done but...'

'But there's the theory and then there's real life,' Morton finished. It was all too easy for the lines to get blurred. Before he'd done undercover work, Morton had imagined glamorous showdowns, secret drug deals to spy on, all-guns-blazing arrests of the biggest names of the criminal underworld. The reality was much drabber: finding an in, breaking minor laws to convince the gang that you were a prospect, and slowly climbing the ranks. There was more time sitting around with other gang members than anything else and the temptation to fill that void with idle chatter often proved insurmountable.

'Exactly. I got confused after one too many drinks out with the gang and mentioned my fiancée. 'cept the gang didn't know jack about Kaylee. They thought I was seeing some bird in the gang and when they offered her their congratulations, I was busted.'

'You didn't try and play it off as a drunken stumble?'

'Of course, I did!' Leon said, swivelling in his chair with restless energy. 'But Tiny Bakowski's much too smart for that. He called me into his office and I knew. "Can't bullshit a bullshitter" he said. And from then on, I was his.'

'Wait,' Morton said. 'This was *before* the press outed you as a dirty cop?'

He hung his head.

'Outed myself, didn't I?' Leon said.

'You outed yourself? Why?'

'Thought it was my best way out of the mess. If the press compromised me, brass would pull me out and Tiny wouldn't have any leverage over me.'

'So why didn't it work?'

'It sort of did. I got fired all right. The polite way. When Superintendent Robinson called me, he had my resignation on his desk all neatly typed up, a biro sitting atop it so I could scrawl my name and get out of there with my dignity intact.'

'And what'd you do then?'

'Everything went quiet. I burned through my savings – and Kaylee's too – until I found this gig. That's when the Bakowskis got back in contact.'

'What did they want?'

Leon turned to the point at the CCTV feed showing the vault. 'Money, of course. And lots of it. And if I couldn't get that, they'd take valuables instead.'

'You gave it to them?'

'Didn't have much choice,' Leon said. 'A bit of cash or my Kaylee's life. That's no decision at all.'

It made Morton pause as he pondered what to do. He had wanted to yell at Leon, to berate him for his idiocy, to castigate him for funding one of London's most dangerous criminal gangs. And yet, had it been Sarah's life that was under threat, Morton couldn't definitively say he wouldn't have done the same.

'How'd you do it?'

'It wasn't hard. A few quid here, a few there. It's not hard to nick stuff when two percent of Crofte's stuff is lost to shrinkage.'

The maths was undeniable. A flagship department store like Crofte's would be turning over millions of pounds of goods a week. Even a tiny fraction could amount to a fortune and the head of security was well-placed to filch whatever he wanted without being seen.

'But how exactly did it work?'

'A burner phone, one of those old bricks we all had in the early noughties. The Bakowksis left it on my doorstep years ago when this all kicked off. It's how I knew they knew where I lived.' Leon said.

'You got it with you?'

He shook his head. 'It's at my place, taped to the bottom of the sofa so Kaylee doesn't see it.'

'Is that the only way that they make contact?'

'Always.'

'Then we need to go get it. No doubt they'll have made some sort of demand.'

'But that's the problem, David,' Leon said. 'I can't get my hands on much these days. Ever since we did a security audit over the summer, management have been watching everyone. Including me.'

He gestured at the screens before continuing. 'These feeds are monitored in real-time from this office. The whole lot is backed up off-site and a security auditing firm reviews all the footage once a month to make sure we're catching everything. I haven't been able to give Tiny a penny in ages.'

'When did you pay him last?'

'The last Sunday in October,' Leon said. 'I'd stolen more than I needed so I had a few thousand in hand. Just in case. Then when that ran out...'

'The threats started?'

It was classic Bakowski behaviour: to extort someone and then, when they weren't useful any more, make an example of them. So why had they only sent Kaylee's ring and not her head? Presumably they still thought Leon could be useful.

'Whenever I get the demands, the sender threatens to hurt her,' Leon said. 'Every single time. He's never followed through before so I've never taken it seriously. But this time, it seems, he means it. It's weird 'cause he didn't do anything in November when I stopped paying him off... I thought he'd finally given up on squeezing me.'

'What was the last message that Tiny sent you?'

'He wants a big payday. From the Christmas takings. A hundred thousand instead of ten.'

Morton whistled. It was an audacious plan. No doubt the store had been heaving for weeks and Christmas Eve was the biggest trading day of the year.

'How much cash will Crofte's take today?'

'Millions, easily.'

'And what did you say?'

'That I'd get caught and that I wasn't doing it. Not that I could: we've got a "two man" system for transferring cash drops. It takes me plus the store manager just to open the vault. In there, he sorts all the takings from the chutes.'

'The what?'

'Chutes,' Leon repeated. 'Each till has a cash chute. Normally, when they get to £500, they put the lot in a canister and put it down their chute. At Christmas we raise the limit to £1000 as it's so busy.'

'Then where does it go?'

'Armoured vans pick it up, two men, and then it's off to the bank. We've got two pickups today, one just after lunch for the morning takings and then another pickup an hour after closing.'

It sounded foolproof.

'Hang on a minute,' Morton said. 'This place is under CCTV lockdown. How the hell did someone sneak in to plant the bloody presents underneath your Christmas tree?'

Leon leant forward, his head almost in his hands. 'Err... about that...,' he mumbled. 'I turned off the cameras.'

'When?'

'Four am this morning.'

'You were going to steal something to try and appease Tiny.'

It wasn't a question.

Leon bit his lip, his head hung even lower. 'Ok. I was. He warned me they'd take her if I didn't come up with a hundred grand by tonight. He said it was my last warning.'

'Who knew you were going to turn off the cameras?'

'Nobody, I swear.' Leon looked up to meet Morton's gaze.

'But someone did find out.'

'Maybe they're watching me?'

A shiver ran down Morton's spine. The idea that the Bakowski brothers – the worst kind of criminal, smart enough to evade capture, dumb enough not to be scared – were watching them – watching him – was terrifying. It had been years since his last chance to put Tiny behind bars. He rued the day that Tiny had slipped through his fingers.'

'Let's not jump to conclusions, Leon. Run me through the timeline of this slowly.'

'I got the message through on the burner.'

'When?'

'Eight-ish last night. They don't usually text then. Most messages come in after midnight.'

'And what exactly did it say?'

'It said "*100Gs or equiv, 5pm tomorrow, usual drop or she dies*".'

'And you assumed that the "she" was Kaylee?' Morton probed.

A small shrug. 'Who else?'

'When they say equivalent, what's that meant before?'

'Gear,' Leon said simply. 'Enough to fence and net a hundred grand. Jewellery, watches, small electronics, caviar, whatever is small and in demand but doesn't have a tracking number on it.'

That ruled out phones with IMEI which were traceable, higher-end jewellery with laser inscriptions on the girdles which could likewise be tracked, and anything else with a similar batch code or identifier.

'So, the CRAVED criteria?' Morton said referring to the infamous police acronym. It meant "Concealable, Removable, Available, Valuable, Enjoyable and Disposable". Goods which ticked all those boxes were the most sought after as they could be flipped for ready cash without losing too large a proportion of the value.

'Pretty much CRAVED plus a size limit. I figure they're collecting the gear in small batches, maybe a car boot full at a time.'

'Makes sense,' Morton said.

'So now what?' Leon asked. 'You still going to call it in?'

The dilemma facing Morton was obvious to both of them. He knew he ought to arrest Leon straight away. He'd confessed to multiple thefts after all. But doing so would almost certainly get Kaylee killed, especially if, as Leon suspected, the Bakowskis were somehow watching them.

Leon looked at him pleadingly. It didn't need to be said again: Morton knew he owed Leon.

'Before I decide, call her mobile, call your land line, just call her. I don't want us to act simply because we found a ring and then find out that Kaylee's still in bed.'

'Alright,' Leon said. 'But it won't do much good. Even if it's on, it might be in Do Not Disturb mode.'

'Humour me.'

Leon complied. Almost immediately, a default recorded message sprang to life: "You've reached O2 voicemail. Please leave a message after the-'

He hung up. 'See?'

Morton frowned. This felt like walking into a disaster but he couldn't risk Kaylee's life.

The fact he was wavering must have been obvious from his expression as Leon tried again. 'Can you risk this not being Tiny? After what he did? Don't you owe it to Sergeant Vaughn to catch him?'

Tiny had eluded Morton for years. He'd fled at the end of one of the most difficult cases of Morton's career, a case that had become personal because Tiny had made it so.

After a brief pause, he knew he had to try. His legal obligations were crystal clear: he was obliged to put the life of a kidnap victim above all else. He debated what cash there might be available in the Met's evidence locker. There was bound to be cash or stolen gear worth a hundred thousand in there that would do nicely by way of ransom. Morton quickly realised the idea was a non-starter: he'd have to convince several other members of the Met's staff to get involved and at least one of them would demand that it all be done by the book instead. That would all take time. Time that Kaylee didn't have. He'd have to borrow what he could from Crofte's and trust that Kieran O'Connor had his back if everything went to pot.

'Given what you said about the vault needing a manager, I'm guessing stealing a hundred grand in cash is off the table even with your ability to disable the CCTV. What goods were you going to take?'

Leon cracked a thin-lipped smile.

'I'm not giving you carte blanche here,' Morton said. 'If – and that's a big if – I agree, I want to take things we can track. And you're paying Crofte's back every penny you've taken when this is all over – even if you have to pay them a tenner a week until you're ninety. Understood?'

'I don't have it all planned. I never expected to nick that much gear in one go. I've got some of it ready but you got here so quick I'm still a way off,' Leon said. 'There's a bunch of low-end gold jewellery in a box on the third floor ready to nab. It'll go for melt value. Then there's a pallet in the corner of the warehouse downstairs which is full of small electrical goods: lasers for hair removal, straighteners, and the like. Nothing with serial numbers. All easy to flog to a market-stall holder or fence online.'

'And you haven't put this in your car because?'

'I was going to do it when I got interrupted by an intruder,' Leon said. 'When I saw the Santa costume, I panicked. I thought we were being burgled at just the wrong moment. It's not insane to think someone else might hit Crofte's on Christmas Eve. Everyone knows we've got extra cash after all but then I saw the box oozing blood and that's when I thought Tiny had finally made good on his threat so I panicked and contacted you.'

It was all a bit, well, convenient. Leon's story made sense from a certain point of view but Morton had never heard of Tiny Bakowski sending in a henchman dressed up as Santa Claus.

'Forget the electronics,' Morton said. 'If we're doing this, we want perfumes and aftershaves, high-end make-up, small and light designer gear, plus the jewellery you've already marked out.'

A rush of adrenaline made Morton shiver. He was, legally-speaking at least, free and clear here. Doing something illegal to save a life wouldn't reflect badly on him. But getting to rob a gigantic department store made him feel like he was on a gameshow he used to love called Supermarket Sweep in which contestants had two minutes to nab whatever they could. There was only one word for it: fun. The goods Morton had chosen to steal while Leon retrieved his boxes were the easiest to flog. If Morton were undercover still, he'd take them to a so-called "level one" fence like a jewellers or pawn broker. From there, the goods would either be sold to the public via a shop or online marketplace like eBay, or they'd get co-mingled with real goods, potentially repackaged, and sold to wholesale markets. It wasn't inconceivable that Crofte's would end up buying back their own pilfered goods.

If Morton got lucky, he could take down a few fences into the bargain.

'I could shut the cameras down again,' Leon said. He glanced at the clock. Time was against them. 'Not for more than ten minutes mind. The cleaners are due to arrive soon and then the footage will look off if people appear in the middle of the store.'

'Fine. When you kill the camera, you grab the jewellery from the third floor. Give me your keys. I'm going to the make-up counter. Where's your car?'

Leon leapt to his feet. 'Downstairs. Basement level two. Are we really doing this?'

'Yep. But bring that UV pen with you. You're signing every item we borrow. And Leon?'

'Yeah?'

'Don't leave it twenty years next time, eh?'

Chapter 3: The Mad Dash

At precisely ten to five in the morning, Leon killed the CCTV. According to Leon, it would take ten minutes for the system to reboot and come back online.

Morton dashed from Leon's office. He had snagged what he thought was the easier job: nicking perfume and beauty products, all of which were located on the ground floor.

The moment he arrived at the row of concession stands, he realised his mistake as he was confronted by a wall of pink and sparkly rubbish. *Bugger,* he thought. He hadn't planned this heist well. He had no idea which brands were valuable and which were not.

In the absence of any real knowledge of luxury women's products, Morton fell back on the old standby: if it sounded French, it was probably as expensive as hell.

Into his basket went Lancôme, Guerlain, Clinique and Estee Lauder. He threw in some Crème de la Mer, whatever that was, and, after glancing at the price tag, nicked some Elizabeth Arden for good measure even though it wasn't French.

Four minutes gone. He had six more to get down to the basement where Leon's car was waiting.

The perfume section saw him on firmer ground as he recognised many of the brands. This time, he ignored the cheaper *"eau de toilette"* and concentrated on pilfering the full strength *"parfum"* bottles made by Tom Ford, Giorgio Armani, as well as more Guerlain. He finished off by grabbing perfumes by two brands he'd never heard of – Maison Francis and Kilian – simply because of the eye-watering price tags.

Two minutes. It was time to get a shift on. He looked up from where he had been frantically scanning the bottom shelf of a large stand full of CREED-branded perfumes. Which way was the damned car park? It took him a moment to orient himself. There, by the fire exit. He jogged over, a clock ticking down in the back of his head. By the time he found himself leaping down the stairs, he probably had sixty seconds left.

Leon had beaten him to it. He was standing by the boot of a banged-up Ford Focus. It was so out of date that the registration plate used the old format. Morton cursed parking his own car across the street: they didn't have time to carry their borrowed goods all the way across the road before the CCTV system came back online.

'Throw it in then!' Leon yelled, pointing at the boot. 'We don't have much time before the CCTV reboots – less than ninety seconds.'

Morton placed his basket in as gently as possible so as not to break any of the glass perfume bottles and then made a beeline for the driver's seat as he was marginally nearer than Leon.

'Keys!'

'It's my car, David,' Leon protested.

'And I'm driving it. Now hand 'em over.'

He did as he was asked, and Morton slid behind the wheel. It was an automatic. Morton pulled a face as Leon got into the passenger side.

'You couldn't have bought a manual?' Morton mocked. 'Or a car from this millennium?'

'Not on ten pounds fifty an hour,' Leon said.

It was barely more than minimum wage and far from enough to comfortably support a family in central London. Morton started the engine, looked over his shoulder to check for any incoming staff, and headed for the exit. Leon pressed a button on his key fob as they approached and the metal gates swung open with a crunch.

'Been keeping a little of the loot for yourself, Leon?' Morton asked as he pulled out into the main road.

'No,' Leon said. 'I'm not like that.'

Morton rolled his eyes and ignored Leon as he fiddled with the satnav. When it had finished booting up, he jabbed the button marked "Home" and an address in Kilburn flashed up. It was four point seven miles away. Assuming there were no traffic incidents, they'd be at Leon's flat in twelve to fourteen minutes depending on how they caught the traffic lights.

'Wait, we can't go to mine,' Leon said.

'How else are we going to verify that your wife isn't sitting at home, safe and sound? She could have lost the ring.' And, Morton thought, if she is, they could return all the stolen goods and nobody would be any the wiser.

'You don't think the Bakowskis will be watching the house? If they see me walking in there with a policeman – and you to boot – they'll kill her in a heartbeat.'

'Then we'd best be subtle about it. You go in, look for any signs of a struggle.' Morton put his foot down, taking the car up to forty miles an hour.

'Oi!' Leon said. 'There are speed cameras all along here.'

'I know.'

'Bastard.'

Morton smirked. 'That's Mr Bastard to you. And a few speeding tickets are the least of your worries.'

'*A few*? How many cameras are there?'

Morton ignored him as they sped along the Edgeware Road, tripping every traffic camera on the way. When they turned onto the A5 northbound, there wasn't a soul on their side of the road. Morton floored it.

It was approaching quarter past five when Morton parallel parked outside the grungy block of council flats that the satnav had directed him to.

'This is where you live?'

'Told you, didn't I? Ten fifty an hour. If I was on the take, I'd have ditched this shit hole long ago.'

'It is a Zone 2 shit hole though, isn't it?' Morton said. 'Not bad for a disgraced detective.'

'The missus pays for most of it,' Leon said. 'You happy now I've told you? I'm a man who can't even afford to pay his own way in life. It's my great shame.'

'Shouldn't be,' Morton said as he killed the engine. 'Nothing wrong with letting a partner pay a bigger share of the bills if they earn more than you. You going to make a move? Any day now?'

'Oh, yeah. Guess I'll be right back.' He opened his door and swung his legs out.

'Don't forget to grab the burner phone. If you're not back in five-'

'You'll come in after me,' Leon said, climbing out as he spoke. The door clicked shut behind him.

'Or wait longer,' Morton muttered.

Chapter 4: A Home Visit

The building appeared to be in exactly the same state as when Leon had left it less than two hours ago. The neighbours were still asleep, not a light shining out onto the street. As he walked along the path up to the front door, it began to snow.

He paused on the doorstep. The communal front door looked untouched. If someone had gone through the door, they'd done so with a key or a very proficient lock picker. He placed his own rusting key in the lock and gently turned. In the stillness of the early morning, the hinges of the door gave a screech that probably carried as far as Morton. With a gentle push, the door swung open to reveal the corridor.

It too looked eerily normal. If Tiny Bakowski had sent someone in, he'd been stealthy enough not to disturb the neighbours, two of whom had their front doors on the ground floor, one to his right and one directly ahead of him. He tried to stop thinking about Kaylee being led out of their home at gunpoint, instead turning to climb the narrow stairway on his left. It wound around and around until he reached the fourth – and top – floor which was divided into two tiny flats under the eaves of the roof. His flat faced the main road which meant he had to contend with the noise of cars whizzing by as well as the risk of whacking his head on the low ceilings. On his front door lay the Christmas wreath that he and Kaylee had decorated the previous weekend with the help of his four-year-old niece. It too was undisturbed.

Surely it was impossible to kidnap someone from a building full of people without being seen and without leaving any physical evidence of the intrusion behind. Even in the dead of night, someone ought to have heard the kidnappers coming and going. Leon knew he had left her sleeping only a few hours ago and so the window of opportunity for a kidnapper to take her hostage, or even just to steal her ring and then drive it over to Crofte's, had to be slim.

He half expected to find her in bed, wondering why on earth he was home early on the most important shopping day of the year. Once again he slowly put his key into the lock, this time using a much-less-grotty stainless-steel key he'd had cut to replace the old one only a few months ago. The door opened in silence, the hall within bathed in darkness. Dare he turn on the light? He didn't want to risk it. The bedroom was on the left. He could imagine her now, half-awake and ears pricked to listen to the sounds in the hallway. Perhaps he should put that light on.

'Hun?' he called out softly.

No reply. She could just be asleep.

He nudged the bedroom door gently open. Still no sound. It was too dark to see anything at all. Kaylee was a light sleeper and had fitted thick, blackout curtains to prevent the pollution from the street lights outside from creeping in.

As his eyes adjusted, he squinted at the bed.

'Hun?' he said again. With one tentative hand outstretched, he shuffled towards the bed. A creak made him freeze. Someone was in the flat.

He leant forward, his arms outstretched. Nothing but duvet. Perhaps it was Kaylee. Perhaps she'd gone to the bathroom across the hall. Perhaps she'd left her wedding ring by the sink as she was want to do when she was cooking and it had simply been pinched from there.

Another creak. He hadn't imagined it.

'Whoever's out there, I'll kill you if you've got my Kaylee.'

A light flickered on in the hallway, temporarily blinding Leon.

'That's no way to say thanks for waking me up at four o'clock in the morning now is it, Leon?'

'Fucking hell, David! I thought you were waiting in the car.'

'It was cold,' Morton said simply. 'And frightfully boring. Besides, if the Bakowskis were watching the house, they'd have seen me outside as easily as they would in here. You ought to learn to shut doors properly behind you, you know. It's not safe around here.'

'Ha bloody ha. Can I assume you've cleared the rest of the flat?'

'Yep, did that while you were shuffling towards the empty bed with your arms outstretched. That was almost worth getting up at four am for. The great Leon Yap, undercover detective turned bed-wandering zombie. There's no sign at all of a break-in. Nothing broken, nothing stained, no blood. You sure she wasn't heading out this morning? No work?'

'Not that I know of,' Leon said. 'Suppose she could have been planning to go Christmas shopping while I was at Crofte's. Then again, we did quite a bit of our shopping together. It's not like we've got spare cash to throw around.'

Morton glanced at his watch. 'Probably a bit early for some Christmas consumerism. She doesn't have a morning jogging routine I take it?'

'Nope.'

'Leon, are you sure she was in bed when you left? You couldn't have just assumed that she was?'

Their bedroom was so dark that it would be possible not to notice someone's absence especially if it was shortly after getting up. Night shifts were often beset by a groggy, slow start.

Leon shook his head adamantly. 'Absolutely not. She *was* there, I know it. Maybe she went under duress. It wouldn't be the first time the Bakowskis simply turned up at someone's door with a gun or a knife and barked orders.'

'Maybe.' Morton sounded doubtful.

'I know what I'm talking about David.'

'I know you do. But how'd they get past the front door?'

'Stolen key?' Leon suggested. 'Or picking the lock?'

'It's a five-point mortis lock. Even this early, someone would have seen them if they'd spent ages picking the lock. That's a main road out there.'

'This is Kilburn. It's a shithole. People wouldn't piss on you if you ran along the street on fire. And the Bakowskis have so many contacts, it wouldn't be hard to find someone that can get through a domestic lock.'

'All while hiding god-knows-where?' Morton said. Tiny had fled the country and his brothers both languished in jail.

'They're smart enough to pull it off.'

'No doubt Tiny is,' Morton said. 'I'm not underestimating him. But this kidnapping took a lot of resources and – no offense – you're just not worth the effort, Leon. You're small fry. How much cash have you been giving him?'

'Ten Gs a month.'

'There you go. He could make that selling crack in an hour. Why would he bother orchestrating a kidnap, having someone rush a ring from here to Crofte's and find a schmuck to dress as Santa to plant the evidence, all to get back a tiny bit of cash?'

He watched Leon like a hawk, searching for any of the visible signs of concealment: excessive stillness, changes in gesticulation, pitch variance, and all the other markers that Dr Jensen taught the Met's officers to look out for. The more that Morton saw, the more he had to wonder if Leon himself was behind Kaylee's disappearance. It was, unfortunately, the most plausible scenario at that point. He had access to the family home, time to concoct the story, and ample opportunity to plant the ring under the Christmas tree. But if Leon was acting, it was a performance worthy of Sir Ian McKellen. His body language was every bit that of a victim in shock.

'I keep thinking the same,' Leon said. 'The Santa suit bothers me. Why dress up like that?'

'Could just be camouflage. Nobody ever thinks Santa is up to no good and even if you did, would you be taken seriously calling 999 to say that you've seen Santa going into a department store? It's ingenious when you think about it. It conceals a lot of the wearer's body shape too.'

'Where do you buy them? Santa suits that is?'

'Could be anywhere,' Morton said. 'Online perhaps. Or even a supermarket.'

'I've seen the supermarket ones. They're cheap and poorly fitting.'

'A costume store then. There's a huge one just off Shaftesbury Avenue as I recall. I bought a Santa costume there once to wear to the Met Christmas party. I'm more interested in the wax hand.'

Leon waved a dismissive hand. 'We've got those all over the store. We use them in our displays.'

Interesting, Morton thought. Did that show familiarity with Crofte's? Had the dodgy Santa cased the joint beforehand? Or was it merely opportunistic?

'And the blood could be from anywhere. I assume Crofte's has a meat counter still.'

'Yep,' Leon said proudly. 'All the best stuff. Hams from Bearfields, joints from TasteTradition, and everything else you could possibly want or need. There's a reason the posh Sloanie types shop with us.'

For a man who'd apparently spent years stealing from Crofte's, Leon was proud of his employers.

'And you've got packaging materials too,' Morton said. 'I saw them on my way in. Everything that Santa needed was already in the building.'

'Except the ring.'

'Indeed.'

Morton leapt to his feet.

'Where are we going?'

'This needs back-up,' Morton said. 'I'm not suggesting we do this on the books but we need to trace your wife's phone and run down any details we can on the burner you've got. You okay with that?'

'Err I guess?'

'Then give me the phone and I'll call in Brodie.'

He disappeared for a moment to fetch it. When he returned Morton promptly put it into an evidence bag and sealed it up. This might be off-the-record but that didn't mean doing things haphazardly.

'Thanks,' Morton said. 'Let's get going then.'

Chapter 5: A Grumpy Scot

A half-asleep Brodie had slouched over half-asleep in his office chair by the time Morton arrived at New Scotland Yard. Leon had been forced to wait the other side of security and so Morton had descended alone into the bowels of the Met where the Digital, Cyber and Communications Department was housed.

Next to Brodie was a vending-machine coffee and a clumsily-assembled bacon buttie. He looked up at Morton with bleary eyes which were almost as red as his hair, clear evidence of a Christmas tipple or two. Had everyone been out drinking last night?

'Morton, ye'd better be paying me treble overtime fer this,' Brodie said. 'It's Christmas Eve.'

'I'm afraid not,' Morton said. 'Did I forget to mention this is a volunteer shift? We're both off the clock today. I'll make it up to you later though. Trust me?'

'Fine,' he said in a tone that suggested it was anything but. 'What do you need?'

Morton produced the evidence bag containing Leon's phone from his pocket and held it out. 'Everything you can get me off of this phone.'

After a cursory examination, Brodie set it down. 'I would'nae hold out much hope, laddie. Tha's a brick o' a phone. Must be almost as old as me.'

'Surely you can find out something?'

'I can pull ye the list o' contacts on it, get a subpoena fer all the records the network has if you'll do the paperwork, and I can send it off fer fingerprints if ye went physical trace.'

'I need something quicker,' Morton said. 'I have reason to believe this phone came from Tiny Bakowski.'

Brodie's eyes lit up. 'The famous gangster? Isn't he off hiding in Portugal or something?'

'Last suspected sighting was in Vigo.'

'Where the feck's that?'

'Arse-end of Galicia,' Morton said. 'It's surprisingly picturesque for Spain's answer to Liverpool.'

He still looked blank.

'Northern Spain.'

'Oh, right,' Brodie said and then quickly steered the conversation back onto more comfortable ground. 'I assume this phone was used fer something specific. Want to tell me what?'

'It's possible that Tiny Bakowski was sending extortion demands to this phone.'

'Via SMS?'

'I presume so.'

'An encrypted app would've been smarter,' Brodie said. 'Wouldn'a big shot gangster like 'im know that?'

The jock had a point. Tiny Bakowski wasn't the kind to expose himself to unnecessary risk.

'Perhaps it was just a henchman that chose and delivered the phone.'

'Mebbe,' Brodie said. 'Let's have a looksee.'

He spun around in his chair to dig through his desk drawer, donned a pair of protective gloves, and then swung back to open the evidence back.

Once his name was scrawled on the evidence log, he opened the bag up and tipped the phone out onto his desk. He powered it up.

'Ah it's a beaut, ain't it? I had one of 'em when I was a kid, played Snake on it for hours,' Brodie said.

It looked like a brick from the nineties, all blue and grey plastic with rubbery buttons backlit in a garish yellow.

'I'll stick to my iPhone, thanks,' Morton said.

'Suit yerself, boss. But this little beauty is virtually unhackable, and it's cheap.'

'You can't help then?'

'Didnae say that, did I? Look, there are dozens of messages on here. They're all from one number.'

Morton read them over Brodie's shoulder. They were all demands for cash, in varying quantities, spaced about a month apart. Each followed the same format.

100Gs or equiv, five pm tomorrow, usual drop or she dies.

Brodie's eyes widened. 'A ransom demand?'

'Indeed. Can you go back a bit? I want to see the oldest messages, the ones where it first starts.'

He scrolled back one:

10Gs or equiv, five pm tomorrow, usual drop or she dies.

Every message was the same. Each included the same death threat. So why had Tiny finally followed through? What made this demand different? The obvious answer was the size of it. Bakowski wanted more money.

But while a hundred thousand pounds was a lot for a security guard like Leon, it was diddly squat for the man who currently occupied the number two spot on Interpol's Most Wanted list. Was there a bigger plan here? Or could it be someone else? One of Tiny's underlings usurping his position now that he was in hiding?

As Morton imagined an up-and-coming gangster turning Tiny's reputation into easy cash, a simpler suspect floated back into his mind. He was still struggling to consider Leon a plausible suspect. Everything he'd seen of his old friend pointed to a man in serious distress, not a master criminal hamming it up. But the evidence was the evidence and it all pointed back to Leon.

'Brodie, can you look up last year's tax return for Crofte's?'

'Nae problem. What're you lookin' fer?'

'I want to know how much they made.'

Brodie's keyboard clicked audibly as he did as Morton asked. 'Looks like they grossed two point one billion and netted a wee smidge under two hundred and fourteen million. Mad, totally mad.'

'Bet most of that was at Christmas too,' Morton said. 'Is there any way of knowing how much they lose to shrinkage each year?'

He tapped away for a few moments. 'Nae, boss, but if it's any good to ya, the mighty Google says the average shrinkage is about one-point-five percent.'

One-point-five percent of two billion. By Morton's maths that meant over thirty million pounds' worth of stock got stolen from Crofte's every year. A hundred grand really was small beer. As much as he wanted to catch Tiny Bakowski once and for all, Morton's gut screamed that this wasn't anything to do with the Ukrainian gangster. A hundred thousand pounds' worth of stock – which might fence for a third of that – was far too little to interest him. Morton also doubted that anyone who knew Tiny would ever double-cross him for such a paltry sum: using Tiny's rep and connections without his authorisation would be seen as a moral sin by the Bakowski Syndicate.

'Thanks for that, Brodie,' Morton said. 'Can you pull a personal tax return?'

He gave a sharp intake of breath. 'Not without a court order and ye won't find that easy ta get on Christmas Eve.'

'What about a credit score?'

'That I can do,' Brodie said. 'Who am I looking up?'

'Leon Yap.'

He didn't recognise the name. Presumably the infamous press fallout was long before the Scot's time. Instead Brodie just typed it into his laptop.

He swung back to face Morton when he was done and leant aside so Morton could peer over his shoulder at the screen.

'Two hundred and twelve.'

'That's pretty dismal, right?' Morton preferred to save first and spend later and so rarely touched his credit cards. There just didn't seem much point in borrowing money for the sake of it especially when he'd been lucky enough to clear the mortgage eons ago.

'Aye,' Brodie said. 'Yer man's had a couple of county court judgements. He hasnae got tuppence to rub together.'

Leon was broke.

Yet again, it pointed back to Leon. Morton's previous ruminations ran rampant in his mind. Leon had access to the store. Leon could easily time a purported kidnapping for a time his wife was away. And it would be child's play to borrow her ring or simply pretend to recognise one that wasn't hers. Everything Morton had to go on was circumstantial and Leon was right in the frame. Even his story – that he saw Santa Claus in his store just when he'd turned the CCTV off – sounded totally made up.

'But why?' Morton mused allowed. Despite the mounting circumstantial evidence, he still couldn't believe it.

'Why what, laddie?'

'Why would a man fake his wife's kidnapping?' Could it simply be that he wanted Morton's help in pilfering a few thousand pounds' worth of goods? Where was the upside? What could Leon ever hope to gain out of all this?

'So that he can pretend to be a "kidnapper", kill her, then watch was we run in circles looking fer a bogeyman?'

Arthur Conan Doyle's words echoed in Morton's mind: *Once you eliminate the impossible, whatever remains, no matter how improbable, must be the truth.*

Brodie's idea was plausible. Before he dashed off to arrest Leon, Morton had to prove it.

'The number that sent the demands—'

'Way ahead of ya, boss,' Brodie said. 'The phone isn't on. It's an unregistered Pay-As-You-Go number.'

'Can you see which towers it connected to last time it was on?'

'Looks like the nearest one was in Brondesbury Park.'

Despite having lived in London virtually his whole life, it didn't ring a bell.

'Where's that?'

'Just west a' Kilburn,' Brodie said having Googled it.

Morton looked at the map on Brodie's monitor. The tower was close to Leon's flat. 'When was this?'

'Half past three this mornin'.'

Right before Leon left for work. It was looking worse and worse.

'Can you tell how the phone was topped up?' Morton asked. There had to be something – anything – that proved it wasn't Leon.

'Nae without calling the network and they'll ask for a court order.'

The same wall. He had no choice but to take Leon into custody.

'Brodie, is there any way to pull CCTV footage from a camera that was turned off?'

Brodie looked at him as if he were crazy. 'If it's off then there's no electricity running through it.'

'Okay,' Morton said. 'What if there was a backup camera or backup generator?' Even as he said it he knew that was clutching at straws.

'*Is* there a backup?'

'No idea.'

'And I thought that I was t' one that needed to go back to bed. Morton, what're you hoping for here? You've got two mobiles, both untraceable burners, and they were in roughly the same spot this mornin' when one phone sent a message to the other. Ye must be thinkin' the same thing t'at I am. Yer friend downstairs is yer prime suspect, inne?'

'Hang on! How'd you know he's downstairs?'

'Our CCTV does work.'

Chapter 6: No Protest

Leon allowed himself to be cuffed without protest. He didn't even say a word as Morton gave him the standard police caution.

What really got to Morton was the expression of sheer disappointment on Leon's face. It was not a look that Morton had ever seen on a guilty man before.

He felt dreadful. On Christmas Eve, he had been forced to accuse an old friend of staging the kidnap of his wife. If he were wrong it would not only have killed an old friendship for nought but it put immense pressure on him to prove Leon's innocence and rescue Kaylee.

When they made it to the interview suite, Morton put on the legally-mandated tape recorder and asked, once again, if Leon wanted a lawyer.

'No,' Leon said. 'I want a friend. But they seem to be in short supply.'

Morton ignored the barb.

'You know why you're in custody.'

'Because you're insane enough to think that I had something to do with Kaylee's disappearance.'

'Did you?'

'No,' Leon said flatly. 'This is so obviously Tiny's handiwork and yet here you are giving him the perfect legal defence – a patsy to point the finger at, and a former policeman at that. Talk about serving up the jury on a silver platter.'

That got under Morton's skin. Not only was Leon inferring he was a bad friend but that Morton was a bad detective too. 'Don't lecture me. You're the one who got fired, and as for not having a friend, you can take that idea and stick it where the sun doesn't shine. Don't forget who answered when you texted them at four o'clock this morning,' Morton said. 'Why did you text me? Why didn't you call and explain what was going on? I could easily have ignored you.'

'I didn't want to give you the chance to ignore me. You'd have told me to phone it in. I knew you'd read the text because you're always on call, and I hoped you'd honour that favour.'

Morton wanted to strangle him. He'd been manipulated into doing something stupid and now he was bang in the middle of a right mess. 'You know that I have no choice but to hold you. The evidence is pretty damning.'

'What evidence?'

Morton listed each bit of the evidence one by one. 'One, you told me you saw Santa Claus plant the evidence. Two, you turned off the CCTV so I can't disprove that nonsense. Three, you admitted to a series of thefts totalling hundreds of thousands of pounds and yet you're so broke that two creditors have obtained county court judgements against you.'

'Being poor's a crime now?' Leon said with a sneer. 'Life ain't roses for all of us, David.'

'Four,' Morton continued. 'The mobile phone that texted you did so from the same cell tower that your phone received it on.'

'Wait, wait, wait. You think I sent *myself* those threats? That's just what Tiny would want you to think. No doubt he had one of his men text from outside while watching me.'

Morton couldn't disprove it. 'Did you see anyone watching you?'

'Well, no,' Leon said. 'But why? Why would I stage a fake kidnapping and then tell *you* of all people? It would be madness.'

'Or a very bold double bluff.'

'Age has made a cynic of you, David. What happened to the good old days?'

'What happened to the good old days,' Morton said, a steely edge creeping into his voice once more, 'is that you sold us out to Tiny Bakowski.'

'And,' Leon said, 'I got away with it. For years. If I were the genius criminal you're suggesting, wouldn't I have just carried on as I was? I didn't need you to help me steal.'

It was beginning to feel like a game of verbal tennis. 'But you would need me to convince the world that you were the doting husband coerced into doing wrong when his wife was kidnapped while in reality, you'd murdered your wife.'

Morton reached over to the tape player and hit pause. 'I can't just take your word on trust any more. Not now I know that the rumours were true. Is there anything, anything at all, that you want to tell me off the record? Give me something tangible to prove it's not you.'

'Nobody can prove a negative, David.'

'Run me through the timeline again,' Morton said. 'We have to have missed something.'

'Okay. I got up at three o'clock. That's an hour earlier than when my alarm always goes off so I was a bit groggy when I got up. Maybe in my stupor I could have missed Kaylee's absence?' He shook his head. 'But I could have sworn I saw her lying right next to me then.'

Even though it was pitch black? 'What next?'

'I grabbed a coffee – I'd made it the night before and kept it ready in my Kinto cup so I didn't have to be noisy – then I grabbed a banana, jumped on my bike and headed-'

'Woah, woah, woah,' Morton said. '*Bike?*' You jumped on your *bike?*'

Confusion reigned as Leon held up his hands in mock surrender. 'Yeah and?'

'We drove your car.'

'Yeah,' Leon said.

He still wasn't following.

'Leon, why was your car in the car park?'

'I'd left it there, hadn't I?' he said, as if it were the most obvious thing in the world. 'I already told you I went out last night after work for a few drinks with colleagues. I left the car in the car park and cycled in this morning so I wouldn't end up driving while drunk.'

It changed everything: Morton's mental timeline was way off. He had assumed a short drive lasting around fourteen minutes without traffic. Cycling in would take twice as long. It opened up a fifteen-minute window that hadn't been there before.

'Can you prove that?'

'Ask my colleagues. Janine – she's the woman who does our window displays – walked back to Crofte's with me at the same time. We had a few drinks in The Botanist after closing. That'd be about six thirty. I was home by eight.'

'Early night.'

Leon lent back in his chair. 'Early start too.'

'Touché,' Morton said. Leon had an answer for everything. It seemed unlikely that he had managed to kidnap his wife without a car. Then again, there was no way to prove when she'd disappeared. Everything relied on Leon's word and right now that was worth about as much as a flying reindeer. Nothing was definitive. It was totally possible that Leon hadn't noticed Kaylee's absence from the flat. It wasn't impossible that someone had merely stolen her ring. According to Brodie, Kaylee's own mobile phone was off but that too meant very little. She could be anywhere, alive or dead, kidnapped or not. Even the identification of "her" ring relied on Leon's word.

It was a Gordian knot and there was just one way to untie it: go to the ransom drop and see who, if anyone, showed up. He told Leon as much and then put the tape back on.

'Leon Yap, I'm remanding you in custody without charge. Interview terminated at six fifty-five am.'

Chapter 7: Reinforcements

Now that Leon was in custody, everything ought to be "by the book".

Except it was Christmas Eve and so the Met was running on a skeleton crew.

Morton had to make do with a dirty compromise: he held Leon on suspicion of murder but without formally charging him. By assuming that Kaylee was already dead, he could keep jurisdiction over the case and run it with his own team.

By nine o'clock, only Rafferty had made it into the building. She was vastly overdressed. Instead of her usual jeans or leggings and a top, she wore a flowing cocktail dress. Her hair, usually sternly tied back or tucked over one shoulder, cascaded down in gentle waves.

'Don't you look posh,' Morton said. 'Going out or coming home?'

'The latter,' Rafferty said. As she spoke, she fished in her handbag. She pulled out a hair clip and began to loop her hair up and behind her.

Thankfully, Rafferty had started "Dry January" a few weeks earlier than everyone else and so Morton didn't need to worry about her sobriety despite the fact she'd obviously been out partying last night.

'Cheers for coming in,' Morton said. 'I owe you one.'

'No big deal,' Rafferty said. She gestured at the empty chair. 'Just the one chair? Who're we waiting for? Ayala or Mayberry?'

'Neither. They're both out of London for the holidays so I'm afraid that chair is for a representative from the AKEU. She should be here any minute.'

'You're letting the Anti Kidnap and Extortion Unit in on this? From what you said on the phone, you didn't think that it was a credible kidnapping.'

'I'm not taking any chances. I want this done as by the book as possible.'

'It's hardly by the book when we're investigating a former colleague, and, in your case, a former friend.'

She had a point. Morton avoided her. 'Have you got a change of clothes in your locker? You won't be able to run in that dress.'

'Will I need to?' Nevertheless, she disappeared out the door without protest.

As Morton waited for her to return, he considered his options. He wished he could hand the whole thing off to the AKEU and head home for Christmas. No doubt by now Sarah was beavering away in the kitchen preparing the Christmas Eve roast lunch which he would probably now miss and not for the first time either. At least Mayberry and Ayala had had the good sense to get themselves far enough out of London that they wouldn't have their Christmases ruined too.

The click-clack of heels striking the concrete floor of the corridor announced the arrival of the AKEU rep. She barrelled into the room causing the door to collide with the wall behind it. Morton winced: there was glass in the frame. Thankfully, it survived the woman's brutality.

At first blush, Morton estimated that she was in her late forties and no more than five-foot-five. She wore a rosary around her neck that draped over to her blouse where it ended in a large silver cross studded with diamonds. Perhaps she wore it to distract from her nose, an upturned bulbous affair that was ill-suited to the round, chubby nature of her cheeks. Combined, the cheeks gave her a piggy look which was only made worse by a long, fringe which acted as curtains for her eyes. As Morton watched her, she swept it aside.

'What the feck are you staring at?' she said.

The woman spoke with a Belfast accent which was both lilting and harsh in equal measure. She had the confident, no nonsense attitude of a woman who'd dealt with bullshit all her life and assumed the worst of everyone she met.

Morton stood to offer a handshake. 'You must be from the AKEU.'

'Aye, Aoife Duffy. And yer Morton, aren't ye? 'bout ye?'

She pronounced her name like "ee-fa". It took an expectant look before Morton realised that "bout ye?" was asking him how he was.

'I'm fine, thanks. Had to come far?'

'A wee way,' Aoife said. 'Going to bring me up to speed?'

'At four o'clock this morning, I was woken up by a text message from Leon Yap, a former colleague who I worked with nearly twenty years ago.'

Aoife pulled out a small, black notebook and began to jot notes in an inscrutably tiny scrawl. 'Why'd you read the message?'

'Force of habit,' Morton said. 'My phone is on during the night precisely because emergencies happen. When I saw Leon's name, I knew something had to be up so I humoured him and did as he asked. I drove straight to Crofte's and parked on the double yellows across the square.'

'Time?'

'I got there about half four.'

'Then what?'

'He explained what he'd found – his wife's ring – and then he told me about the extortion demands that he's been receiving.'

'How long for?'

It was a good question. 'You'd have to ask him that. I presume since he left the police.'

'Never assume.' Aoife said. Just as Morton was about to hit back that he too was an experienced detective, she jabbed her pen in his direction. 'Carry on.'

'He said that he'd been paying up to avoid Tiny Bakowski's wrath. Each month he'd been stealing around ten thousand pounds' worth of gear. That stopped in September when Crofte's tightened up their security. Since then, he's received the same ten grand a month demand right up until this month's sudden escalation to asking for one hundred thousand pounds. Throughout all the messages, the threat has been the same: hand over the cash or we'll kill Kaylee. He hadn't taken that seriously until this morning when he found her ring.'

'I don't buy it,' Aoife said dismissively, setting her pen down as she spoke. 'Your timeline doesn't add up.'

'How so?' Morton said, straining to remain polite.

'Your victim leaves his wife, gets to work for when exactly?'

'He arrived at four having left at half three.'

'Right, so someone kidnapped her *after* half past three when he left home but *before* half past four when the pair of you found her ring in the box. How far is Leon's house from Crofte's?'

'It took us roughly fifteen minutes without traffic,' Morton said. 'It's possible.'

'Possible doesn't mean probable,' Aoife said. 'You're assuming your friend is telling the truth.'

'He's not my friend.'

She glared. 'Then why did you pause the tape while interviewing him?'

Morton said nothing. He hadn't realised she'd listened to the tape before coming up to the incident room. Perhaps that was why she'd taken so long to come into the incident room.

'Chief Inspector, you're playing a dangerous game here. I know you feel loyal to a former colleague but my job is to get Kaylee home safely. Are we on the same page?'

She was right. The law was clear: life and limb came before evidence and arrest.

'So, what do we do?'

'*We* do nothing,' Aoife said. 'I'm going to interview Leon again. You missed things.'

'Such as?'

'You didn't ask a single question about the victim,' Aoife said. 'Not one. How was she abducted? Why would she answer the door at half three in the morning? In Kilburn of all places?'

'Perhaps she thought it was Leon coming back?' Morton suggested. 'It isn't inconceivable he could have forgotten his keys and turned around to get them. In her half-asleep state, she answers the door thinking its him and instead finds Tiny's henchman on the doorstep.'

'And how did the henchman get in?'

'He could have tailgated Leon.'

'Got an answer fer everythin', don't ye?' Aoife said. 'And how did she get kidnapped without a neighbour hearing her?'

'Perhaps her abductee had a knife or a gun,' Morton said. 'Or maybe the neighbours did hear but were half-asleep and didn't think anything of it. If an abductor acted swiftly with the benefit of surprise, they could have had her gagged and bound in seconds.'

Aoife looked doubtful. 'Maybe.'

'It's possible.'

'Aye, and it's possible that Idris Elba's going to come and sweep me off my feet for a Christmas Eve breakfast.' She looked at the door expectantly as if he might burst in at any moment. 'Shame. Guess I'll have to settle for yer vending machine butties.'

'Then what's your case theory?'

'He did it. He killed her whenever, kept the ring. This morning, he went to work, turned off the CCTV, planted the ring, texted you with the cockamamie bollocks about seeing Santa, and you've fallen for it hook, line, and sinker.'

Leon hadn't, in fact, said anything in his text to Morton but Aoife didn't need to know that Morton owed Leon his life. She already thought that Morton was too quick to defend him. 'Evidence?'

'Horses, not zebras. It's the simple explanation. Think about it. You saw their bedroom. How big was it?'

'Not big.'

'King size bed?'

'Double. I think.'

'And it's all old stuff?' Aoife asked. 'Soft, sagging mattress?'

'What're you getting at?'

'Folks roll together. Yer vic's a big lady. I Googled her. Leon ain't slim himself. Put those two chubsters on a saggy double mattress and they're gonna roll right into t' middle. No way in hell is he going to be able to leave without noticing if she's there or not.'

Morton took a sip of coffee as he processed what she was saying. It made sense. 'Okay. Then she had to be there. That doesn't contradict my timeline.'

'No, but it makes a liar of yer friend. And winnows down the timeline for your case theory to the point that everything would need to be planned to the last second. They'd need to see Leon leave, get a foot in the door jam without him turning around to see 'em, get inside, creep upstairs, abduct her and then, here's the hard part, get her out of the building and take them with her to plant the ring.'

'Them?'

'It'd have to be a team, Chief Inspector,' Aoife said. 'One to keep her hostage, another to don the Santa suit and plant her ring underneath the tree. Never mind how hard it would be to get into Crofte's after also breaking into the Yap residence. See why I'm sceptical?'

'Unless the ring was done in advance and then the kidnappers took her any time after Leon left but before we returned. That's more manageable.' 'But they still had to be at Crofte's right when Leon turned off the CCTV.'

Bugger. She was right.

'I'm going to send Rafferty – my DI – to canvass the neighbours,' Morton said. 'Someone must have heard something.'

'No, yer not,' Aoife said.

'Why on earth not?'

'Because I already sent her.'

Morton felt his fingers clench as his patience ran short. 'You had no right.'

'I have every right,' Aoife said. 'This is your city, your team. But this is my life. How many hostages have you negotiated the safe return of? How many times have you been on the wrong end of a shotgun in the middle of the Troubles? If it's possible to do, I'm going to get your hostage back safely. And I'll do my damndest to nail the bastard who did this. If justice is what you want, we're on the same team so how about a truce? Til five o'clock tonight anyway.'

'Til five o'clock.'

Chapter 8: The Denizens of Kilburn

This wasn't a part of London that Rafferty was overly familiar with. Despite its proximity to wealthy Hampstead to the east and the even wealthier Kensington to the south, Kilburn felt like an enclave of acute poverty. The houses were run down, the cars older than Rafferty, and the peeling paintwork on the frontage of Leon's building was a portent of the interior.

There were, unsurprisingly, no CCTV cameras. With most of Kilburn owning nothing worth stealing, Rafferty knew that such a camera would be a magnet for thieves looking for rich pickings.

The building itself wasn't particularly large. It was sandwiched between two other developments almost like an afterthought. Here nobody had taken the time to salt the icy pavement and so Rafferty followed a narrow path from the road where the ice had melted due to foot traffic.

Judging from the number of buzzers by the communal front door, Leon's building was divided up into six units. She drew Leon's key from her pocket and let herself in. It was as manky inside as she expected. In the cold light of day, she could see just how dusty and worn the floorboards were. She made her way up to Leon's top-floor flat, taking note of which neighbours had lights on so she could return to them afterwards.

As she approached the front door, Rafferty noticed how old it was. Years of scratches had layered upon each other to create an intricate pattern in the dark green paintwork. The gouges were particularly bad around the keyhole as if someone had tried to let themselves in while the hallway light was off.

The keys jangled as she tried to work out which key was for Leon's front door. Leon had three keys on his keyring, none of which were labelled. She noted that, unlike his next-door-neighbour, Leon hadn't installed a peephole.

Inside she felt in the dark for a light switch. An ancient bulb flickered to life to reveal a minuscule flat. The bedroom door to her left was wide open, the bed within taking up nearly the entire room. Ahead of her was a small kitchen-cum-living room with dormer windows on which she could see a thin film of condensation. There was black mould around the edges of the frames that was thick enough that Rafferty could see it from the hallway.

It was as Morton had described. Nothing appeared to be broken but the place was such a mess that Rafferty wasn't confident she'd be able to tell if something was. Once she'd had a quick look around the living room for anything that Morton might have missed during his brief visit, she made her way into the bedroom and laid on the bed in accordance with the instructions that Aoife had texted. It was a weird request but one Rafferty didn't mind complying with.

The bed was, as Aoife had expected, knackered. It sagged badly in the middle. She texted back to confirm as much and then, with a great struggle, hauled herself back to her feet while being mindful of the sloping ceiling. The only storage in the room was a small Ikea chest of drawers which held an assortment of clothing. On top was a small stack of paperbacks, a mix of crime thrillers and bodice rippers. Just in case, Rafferty continued to search the flat for any stolen gear. When she found none, she backtracked to the hallway to interview Leon's neighbours.

There was no light creeping out from underneath the door across the hall. Rafferty knocked anyway. Nada. She tried again and then, when nobody answered, slipped one of her business cards under the door on the off-chance they might call.

She had more luck downstairs though it still took several minutes of knocking to get somebody to answer the door. The door cracked open, still on the chain. The man who answered was elderly, perhaps in his seventies, with a wizened face and small suspicious eyes.

'Hi, I'm Detective Inspector-'

'ID?' he demanded.

She showed him and he visibly relaxed. 'Just a mo,' he added as he shut the door. It opened again, this time off the latch. 'Sorry about that, luv. Can't be too careful around here. What can I do ya for?'

'What can you tell me about your upstairs neighbours, Leon and Kaylee Yap?'

'Oh ho, you'd best come in luv. Barb! Oi, Barb! We've got company. Stick the kettle on!'

A woman's voice shouted back. 'Stick it on yourself, you lazy old-'

The woman, who Rafferty assumed was Barb, appeared in the hallway behind her husband and froze when she saw Rafferty in the doorway. 'Oh, hello.'

'Hi. I'm Detective Inspector Rafferty. I'm sorry to disturb you.'

Barb flashed a toothy smile. 'Not at all dear, not at all. Jack, you put the kettle on and I'll show Mrs Rafferty here to the living room.'

She nudged Jack out of the way. 'Through there dear.'

Jack and Barb's living room was the polar opposite of Kaylee and Leon's. Where Leon lived in squalor, mess everywhere, Jack and Barb had everything meticulously arranged. Photos of children

– presumably grandkids – were arranged at right angles on the mantlepiece. There wasn't a speck of dirt or dust to be seen anywhere.

Two small sofas were bedecked in blankets in a duck egg blue colour reminiscent of Tiffany and Co. Between them was a low coffee table made of burred walnut atop which sat a large doily.

'Sit down then, dear.'

Rafferty perched on the edge of one sofa.

When Barb had sat down too, Rafferty started again. 'Do you know Leon and Kaylee well?'

'Oh yes, I've known Leon since he was a boy. That old flat was his parents' place before it was his. They're gone now, bless their hearts. Lovely folks. His Daddy was a copper too.'

'And Kaylee?'

Barb paused as if unwilling to speak ill of someone who wasn't there to defend herself. 'Not so well, that one.'

'Do you know what she does for a living?'

'She's an accountant, dearie.'

Jack reappeared in the doorway carrying a teapot, three cups, and a packet of digestive biscuits. He guffawed. 'Like heck she is. That girl couldn't count her way out of a paper bag.'

'Well, that's what she told me. Said she worked in the City.'

'I've seen her down the Red Lion during the day. Not many accountants that nip out for a pint in their Kilburn local, are there?'

'Well, she's always got money. That car of hers-'

Rafferty leapt in. 'What car?'

'She's got one of those new CLA Coupés. I think she said it belonged to work. She parks it next door at the fancy development. I think someone rents her their space?'

It seemed odd. A brand-new Mercedes like that was worth at least thirty grand, a year's salary for many Londoners. While it might be a perfectly good choice for a company car, it didn't quite jive with the squalor that Leon and Kaylee lived in.

She pulled out her phone as Jack sat down next to his wife and began pouring the tea. 'Sorry to be rude but I need to ask a colleague to check something.' She typed in the name Brodie and hit send message.

Brodie, can you find out where Kaylee works and if she had a company car. Ta. – Ashley

Rafferty put the phone back down.

'Did either of you hear anything out of the ordinary this morning?'

Barb looked to Jack. 'I don't think so.'

'Nor me, Barb,' Jack said. 'When are you talking about?'

'Between half three and four o'clock.'

'Nope,' Jack said firmly. 'Nothing comes to mind.'

'No screaming, no banging, no strange noises that you thought were part of a dream?'

Barb shook her head. 'None of that, dear. He's a very light sleeper. Anything more than the quietest of footsteps in the hallway and Jack bolts upright. Me, I could sleep through a hurricane. I know because I still remember the devastation of that hurricane back in eighty-seven.'

Rafferty stood, her tea untouched. Jack and Barb looked sorry to be losing their guest so quickly.

'One more thing, have you ever seen Leon show off a lot of money?'

Another head shake. 'No dear. Poor boy's not got tuppence to rub together.'

Chapter 9: Gentle Prodding

While Morton watched from the other side of the one-way glass, Aoife sat down opposite Leon in Interview Suite One. He looked at her blankly.

'Who might you be?' he asked,

'Detective Inspector Aoife Duffy. I'm the SIO assigned to your wife's case on behalf of the Anti-Kidnap and Extortion Unit.'

Leon swore. 'I told him not to bloody call it in.'

'He did the right thing, Leon,' Aoife said. 'I've heard your side of the story from Morton.'

'And now you want to hear it from the horse's mouth.'

'Nope. I want to ask a few more questions. We're running out of time here. Tell me how the drops worked.'

'I stole. I drove. I delivered.'

'Where'd you take the deliveries?'

'There's a derelict house on Granville Road. with a basement garden that can't be seen from the road. I leave the gear there, it disappears by morning.'

'How much stuff?'

'Ten grands worth...' At this look on her face, Leon added. 'Oh, physically? Never more than I can fit in the boot of my car.'

'Ever tried watching for a pickup?'

'Once,' Leon admitted. 'A few months in. I sat in my car and watched from the end of the road. When I did that, nobody turned up. I figured they'd seen me.'

'What happened next? Did you leave the stolen goods there?' Aoife asked though she knew the answer. Brodie had already procured complete text logs.

He leant forward as if imploring her to believe him. 'When I went to get the gear, it was gone. Guess I missed 'em somehow.'

It wasn't a road Aoife was familiar with. 'Is there any way they could have come and gone unseen? And did anyone know you were planning on watching them that night?'

'Through the house maybe? And nah, nobody 'cept the missus knew a thing. Had to explain where I'd gone as otherwise she'd have had a fit.'

Aoife sat upright. 'Kaylee knew about the threats?'

'Sorta,' Leon said, shifting uncomfortably in his seat. 'I had to tell her something, didn't I? So, I told her I had gambling debts and that I had to pay somehow.'

'And she went along with that?'

'She wasn't happy about it. Better to nick a few quid than get knee-capped though, that's what I always told her.'

Aoife felt her phone buzz in her pocket. She pulled it out and surreptitiously read all the messages. The last one was from Morton. He wrote:

Abandoned house checks out. There is one on Granville Road. Met database shows several fly tipping incidents in the area.

She flicked backwards to the older messages. One was from Detective Inspector Rafferty confirming that there was indeed a soft, old double bed as Aoife had expected. She honed in on that.

'You loved your wife, didn't you Leon?'

He paled. 'Loved? Past tense? She's not dead, is she?'

Before Aoife could reply, he'd leapt to his feet and begun to pace the tiny interview room.

'Sit down, Mr Yap. I didn't say she was dead.'

'Then why'd you use past tense?'

'Because I want to know if you still love her.'

He sat down and pulled his chair in. 'O' course.'

'Then why weren't you sharing a bed?'

'What? How... Why'd you think that?'

'Your bed is a double. It's exceptionally worn and soft. They're not supposed to last decades after all. If you'd been sleeping in it with Kaylee last night, you'd have been pressed up against her and would have known she was still there when you left. I'll ask you one more time. Why were you sleeping on the sofa?'

He hung his head. 'Because we can't afford a new mattress. It's too saggy. I sleep on the sofa so we don't end up squidged up in the middle every night, okay? It's nothing to do with our relationship. I still love her.'

But does she love you? Aoife wondered. 'What does Kaylee do for a living?'

'She's an accountant.'

'Impressive. She must be a smart woman. How long's she been doing that?'

'Since I left the Met.'

'Since you were *fired* from the Met,' Aoife corrected him. 'That can't have done much for your ego. First you disgrace yourself and then you sit back like a pansy and let your wife earn the money. What do your friends say about that?'

Leon slammed his fists on the table, his handcuffs clanging against the table. 'How fucking dare you!'

'Then again, maybe you don't have any friends. But you do have quite the temper, don't you Leon? Did you kill her?'

He sneered. 'No, I bloody didn't. You think you're so bloody smart, don't you? First thing they teach you when you become a cop isn't it? Look at the spouse. Well, you're wasting your time. And mine. Lawyer. Now. Get out.'

Chapter 10: Tick Tock

'That went well,' Morton said the moment Aoife emerged into the hallway.

She flashed him a smile. 'It did, didn't it?'

'Was I watching the same interview? He's lawyered up. By the time the duty solicitor gets here and takes his brief, we'll be past the five o'clock ransom drop.'

'Exactly.'

'You provoked him on purpose.'

'Of course, I did. He stays where he is. We go to Granville Road and prove his story's a load of crock.'

'And if you're wrong, Ms Duffy?' Morton said. 'What if Leon didn't do it and we're leaving Kaylee in the hands of one of Bakowski's clowns? Didn't you say your number one priority was getting her back?'

'She's dead as a door nail, David. I've seen men like him before. He's quick to anger. He's proud. A menial job in a department store won't sit well with his ego.'

That bit, at least, was true. But it didn't mean he'd killed her. 'So why would he kill her now? Why today? They've been together for years. What spurred him to act in your mind?'

She shrugged and began to walk along the corridor. 'Not my job. That one's on you.'

Morton followed. 'You haven't proved a thing. So what if he slept on the sofa? That makes his story more believable not less. He'd have no reason to have checked in on Kaylee before he left. She could've disappeared any time after he went to sleep in the lounge.'

'So now you think someone abducted her while he was fast asleep on the sofa? That she answered the door in the middle of the night, was forcibly removed at gun or knife point, and he snored all the way through it?' Aoife scoffed. 'You want your friend to be innocent. The evidence isn't looking good. We have to keep him in custody.'

'I agree,' Morton said, much to her surprise. 'But that doesn't mean we twiddle our thumbs and wait for five o'clock.'

'What do you have in mind?'

He told her.

Chapter 11: Tracing

Morton quickly put the team to work. Rafferty was already halfway back from Kilburn so Morton asked her to divert back to Crofte's. Someone needed to explain to the store manager that their head of security was assisting with a police investigation and wouldn't be in today. Brodie was off doing whatever it was that tech nerds did. Hopefully he'd dig up a bit more on their victim.

Meanwhile, he and Aoife had seized on the only physical evidence they had: the goods that Leon had stolen in previous months. Leon had a good memory and so, after a brief off-the-record chat, they found themselves in the hallway outside Interview Suite One with a scribbled note of everything that Leon could recall about the goods that he had dropped off in August, September, and October.

It read:

August: Meat, caviar, wine, champagne, cheese.
September: Perfume, make-up, video games, consoles.
October: Jewellery, champagne.

'What exactly do you intend to do with this?' Aoife asked.

'Simple,' Morton said. 'Find the stolen goods, interview the fence. If we know who sold the gear, we can prove whether or not Leon was involved.'

'Need I remind you that it's Christmas Eve?' Aoife said. 'How're you going to run down where this lot went several months after the fact?'

It would be a challenge. The first step was to try and verify that Leon's recollection was correct. Then they'd need to work out how a criminal would try and dispose of each of the stolen goods.

'Morton? Are you listening to me? It'll be long gone. Both the meat and cheese are perishable.'

'Huh?' Morton snapped out of his reverie. 'True, true. But the rest isn't. Chances are, the disposable stuff was fenced to a grocery store or restaurant.'

'And how many restaurants and corner shops are there in London?'

'Thousands,' Morton conceded. 'But not many of them sell caviar. You're right though, the food is a needle in a haystack.'

'And the other stuff? Isn't that just as hard to trace?'

'Chances are the video games have gone to one of those electronics stores that takes trade-ins. That's the easy way to get rid of bulk. I'll have Brodie check online auction sites too.'

'For what? Any video games sold? Leon can't even remember exactly what he stole and in what quantity.'

Morton waved a dismissive hand. 'Now we have a good general idea, Rafferty can liaise with Crofte's to go through their stock and look for theft beyond their usual level of shrinkage. They know what they've bought in and what they've sold so they should be able to work out what's missing.'

Chapter 12: Shopping Mania

The manageress of Crofte's was none too happy about Rafferty's arrival. Not only had she insisted on calling the Met switchboard to verify Rafferty's identity but she'd then spent the better part of an hour tucked away in her office presumably attempting to get hold of the department store's owner or possibly even the store's lawyer.

She emerged from her office and into the hallway where Rafferty had been sitting twiddling her thumbs. Before she said a word, Rafferty knew that whatever call she'd made hadn't gone well.

'Miss Bonaparte, before you turn me down, think about it. I could come back in an hour and shut you down for the rest of the Christmas Eve. That won't play well with your customers.'

'No need for the threats, detective. The problem isn't our willingness to help but the fact that we don't keep everything on one centralised database. It isn't something I can just conjure up because you asked. I'll let you see what records I have on-site.'

'But?'

'But I'm afraid it won't do you much good. A lot of our stock gets stolen. That's the nature of the beast when you run a department store. That will throw off the numbers a bit because you've no way of knowing what our former head of security stole and what was taken by general shoplifters.'

'You're firing him then?'

'Naturally,' Bonaparte said. 'As to the information you seek, it sounds like your best bet will be to talk to the manager of our jewellery department. The theft of jewellery involves the highest value items on a per item basis and we suffer very little shrinkage to shoplifters because everything is kept under lock and key. I have taken the liberty of sending for him. He'll be with you in any moment. Good luck, detective. If you do somehow manage to recover our goods, would you give me a call?'

She thrust a business card at Rafferty. It was a thick, weighty card, the kind that was reassuringly expensive. Her name was written in gold ink on a near-black background. By the time Rafferty had turned it over, Bonaparte was gone.

A few more minutes passed as Rafferty waited for the jewellery department manager to make an appearance. After another five minutes of twiddling her thumbs, Rafferty gave up on waiting for her and headed downstairs. The public stairwell was rammed with shoppers shuffling up and down, most of them laden down with a basket or collection of carrier bags. As she descended, she glanced in on each floor starting with kitchenware on the fifth floor. It was bedlam and the crowds grew progressively bigger with each floor. No doubt the ground and first floors, which contained the food hall, cosmetics, and clothing departments, would be the worst of the lot. On the third floor, bedlam turned to an eerie stillness as a large barrier had been placed across the entrance to the jewellery department with a sign that read "temporarily closed" hanging from the middle of the rope.

She ducked under the barrier and made a beeline for the tills where three people, one of whom was clearly in charge. They were arguing about something. The three looked over as Rafferty approached. She flashed her warrant card.

'Inspector Rafferty?' asked the manager. 'I'm Elias Van Hess. I manage this section of the store. Could you give me a few more minutes? I'm trying to pull the records you asked for. As you can see, it is proving problematic.'

Rafferty leant on the checkout and craned her neck to take a peek at the monitor. 'Why is that?'

'This is not – as it looks – one shop. Each of these areas' – Hess pointed at sections of the floor in turn, each with its own branding – 'belong to an external concession. As each franchise runs its own proprietary system, it is not easy to reconcile each and I must ask the permission of the franchise owners before I can even try to do so.'

'Which,' Rafferty said, 'is presumably rather difficult on Christmas Eve.'

'Exactly.'

'What information can you give me right now? Surely the whole floor isn't franchised?' There were great swathes of the jewellery department which were branded in Crofte's black and green livery.

Hess gave up fighting with the point-of-sale machine, left his two colleagues to continue fighting it, and walked around the till to Rafferty. 'You're right, of course. Everything that isn't part of a branded concession is ours. The thief took mostly mid-range products.'

'What's mid-range?'

'It's our in-house term for quality jewellery that isn't from a famous designer. It doesn't include the high-end stuff – Atelier Swarovski, Annoushka, Stephen Webster and the like – nor does it include any of the "fashion" brands which might use low-grade, synthetic, or even simulant gemstones.'

'What's the difference?'

It took Hess a moment to realise what Rafferty was referring to. 'Low-grade stones might be included or treated in some way. For example, ruby might be "fracture filled" with glass, emeralds are usually oiled, tanzanite heated, topaz irradiated and so on and so forth. These cheaper stones are also usually "native cut" which means all the cutting was done at the mine on the cheap.'

'And this is relevant because...?'

'Because it won't sell for much. The value for a thief is just in the gold. A ring might be two or three grams and the nine-carat stuff is thirty-seven-point-five percent pure gold. Melt it down, you've about a gram in a typical ring.'

'Worth?'

'At today's spot price, thirty pounds.'

It was a lot of work for thirty quid. A thief could get more by stealing from an unguarded backpack or purse. 'And the others?'

'The simulants,' Hess said, 'are worthless. These are the "substitute materials" like the cubic zirconia earrings you're wearing right now.'

Rafferty tucked a strand of hair behind her ears self-consciously.

'How'd you know?'

'It looks cheap,' Hess said. 'And it's often set in silver or gold-plated silver. Real jewellery usually uses eighteen carat gold, platinum, or, occasionally, palladium. It's the synthetic gems that prove problematic. They're made in a lab but are chemically identical to the real thing. The only way you can tell is if you send the stones off to a lab to look for chemical impurities... and they're faking those these days too.'

Chemically identical? 'So, what's the point in buying the real deal?'

'Prestige,' Hess said. 'They cost more, they're rarer, people ascribe social value to those attributes. I personally like the synthetics. They cost a fraction of their mined counterparts and no children get hurt in the process.'

'Children? Aren't there labour standards for miners?' Rafferty flashed back to what she'd read about the Kimberley Process.

'Indeed... but they're not consistent or consistently applied.'

'This is all interesting but how can I use this?'

He led her over to a display of thick, gold chains. They looked fancy.

'See this? Guess how much it costs.'

Rafferty examined it. There was an Italian brand name she didn't recognise hall-marked on the clasp. A smaller font identified is as being "18k WG" meaning that it was three-quarters pure white gold. Beyond that, all she had to go on was the heft.

'Five grand?'

Hess laughed. 'Fifteen thousand, eight hundred retail.'

'It's worth that?'

'Second hand?' Hess said. 'Maybe half if you can prove its provenance. But if you melt it... then a Luca original gold bracelet is just twenty grams of scrap metal.'

Rafferty did the maths. Twenty grams, 18k, thirty quid a pop. 'Four hundred and fifty quid?'

'Minus your smelting costs and any middleman's markup. Not much of a return. It takes a trained and practiced eye to see the beauty and value in people.'

It sounded as if it took self-importance but Rafferty didn't dare say as much. 'That doesn't sound like Leon.'

'Mr Yap was... not our kind of people. He would not have known how to spot the difference. The synthetics were on public display because they are easily replaceable. The best jewellery was rarely on public display and we keep all of the paperwork – without which a designer ring is just a ring – in a separate lockbox to which only I and my assistant manager have access. We're confident Mr Yap didn't steal any designer pieces. It's most likely that he took the nicer-looking mid-range gems and the synthetics. The latter, to the untrained eye, look more expensive than the former.'

'Hang on, Leon stole *fakes*?'

'Synthetics,' Hess corrected her. 'Not fakes. Whoever bought the stolen jewellery from him is in for a nasty shock if they ever send it to a lab for analysis.'

'Will they?'

'Unlikely,' Hess said. 'It's probably going to be melted down or sold to some unsuspecting consumer as the real deal. These criminals are not sophisticated. They steal a ring worth a thousand pounds, pop the gemstone out and melt the mount itself down for scrap.'

'Wouldn't they get more if they kept it as one piece?'

He nodded. 'Undoubtedly. That carries a risk. To sell to the public, they'd need a storefront. We monitor all the online marketplaces for our stolen goods – as most retailers do – as part of our stock recovery efforts. Mr Yap would undoubtedly have known that.'

Leon might have known that... but would the blackmailers? If it were one of Tiny's lackeys, not the big man himself, they may have tried to sell the pilfered jewellery rather than melt it.

'Thank you, Mr Hess. How long until you have a better idea of what's missing?'

He spread his hands apologetically. 'I'm afraid I do not know. It could be hours. Or days.'

Rafferty glanced at her watch. They had less than three hours left until the ransom was supposed to be dropped off. All she had learned so far backed up Leon's story: he had stolen jewellery in October as he had claimed. They now had a slightly better idea of what they were looking – and mere hours in which to turn that into the lead they so desperately needed to find in order to bring Kaylee home alive.

She texted Morton with her findings.

***

It was as Morton had suspected: Leon had grabbed whatever he could and hoped for the best. Morton relayed Rafferty's discoveries to Aoife who was sitting at the opposite end of the conference table in the incident room. Brodie sat halfway down the table, earphones in, his eyes transfixed on the laptop in front of him as if he were paying no heed to the bickering detectives. Morton knew otherwise: he could see the tech trying to suppress a smile.

'Surely you agree now that Leon wasn't doing this professionally?' Morton said. 'If this was all him, he'd have taken the time to learn what did and didn't sell. Taking synthetics isn't the mark of an experienced thief.'

'Being thick isn't a bar to being a criminal.'

A sudden anger flooded through Morton. 'You're suggesting he's too thick to Google what's worth stealing but smart enough to get away with pilfering goods for a decade and then again smart enough to taunt us by, according to your theory, killing his wife before involving me to try and make it look like a kidnap. Pick your poison, Aoife. You can't have it both ways. What's his game plan? He must have known that I'd have to bring him in as a suspect.'

'He's playing you, Morton,' Aoife said, 'like a god-damned fiddle. He's dangled the spectre of Tiny Bakowski in front of you and you're lapping it up. The world's most infamous gangster turns up at Christmas and is immediately handed to the detective who's wanted to catch him for years? Get real. It's a sop to your ego. You just want to catch Tiny, prove your friend is innocent, and go home to Christmas with your family.'

'Of course, I do!' Morton said. 'Of course, I want to catch him. But I know it's not Tiny. I never thought it was, just that it could well be someone related to the Syndicate.'

'Then who fences for the Syndicate?' Aoife demanded. 'If it's that easy, show me where the stolen goods went.'

'That's the best question you've asked all day. I assume you agree that we ought to focus on the jewellery.'

'Aye. It's the most recent, the most valuable, and it won't have been consumed like the meat and wine.'

'Then we need to find out who has been nicked for receiving stolen goods in the vicinity of Kilburn. Brodie? Brodie, you can stop pretending you're not eavesdropping now.'

The burly Scot yanked his earphones out. 'Huh? Were ye talking to me?'

'Give it up, Brodie,' Aoife said. 'We all knew you were listening. Fences for jewellery with connections to north west London-'

'Or the Bakowski Crime Syndicate.'

'Right, yer, I'll have a look.' Brodie had obviously already started. In less than five minutes, he'd connected his laptop to the projector to show them everything he had found.

Brodie waved an arm at the screen. 'Along this stretch of the A5 running south of Brondesbury Station down into Maida Vale, there are no fewer than twenty-two pawn shops and jewellers. All bar one of 'em have been investigated by us for receiving stolen goods.'

'Twenty-two?' So much for looking for a needle in a haystack. This was looking for a needle in the toilets of Fabric nightclub on a Saturday night.

'Aye and six of 'em are being watched the be Serious Organised Crime boys for funding gang crime. Want me to start with them?'

'Please.'

'The largest of the jewellers – Gerrard's – is run by an Irish chap that's been in and out of prison since he was in nappies. I'd say it's a damned good bet he's been handling stolen goods.'

'If he is, he'll be running a tight ship,' Morton said. 'When was his last stint?'

'Four years ago. And get this, he was on the same wing as Tiny Bakowski's younger brother.'

Four years was a long time. Either Gerrard had gone clean... or he'd been careful. Morton would have bet his life on the latter. 'Where's he live?' Morton demanded.

Brodie tapped away at his keyboard for a few minutes. 'Queen's Park.'

Morton leapt to his feet closely followed by Aoife.

'Then let's pay Mr Gerrard a visit.'

Chapter 13: On the Fence

They drove over in silence. As Aoife scrolled through something on her phone, Morton wove in and out of the Christmas Eve traffic on the short hop to Queens' Park. It was southwest of Leon's home and in a much more affluent area. Gerrard's address was on file as being on Milman Road on the western edge of the park itself, a road full of tall imposing Victorian terraces with large bay windows and dormer loft conversions dotted amongst the rooftops. The house looked remarkably homely. A Christmas tree with presents was visible in the window while the roof was bedecked with rope lights, a dozen plastic reindeers and a ginormous sleigh.

'Nice,' Aoife said, finally breaking the silence as they emerged from Morton's Audi. 'Perhaps crime does pay after all.'

'If it didn't,' Morton said sadly, 'nobody would ever commit crime. Come on, let's go interrupt Gerrard's Christmas.'

It took several knocks for the jeweller to answer the door. When he did, Morton was taken aback. He had expected to see a hardened career criminal, a skinhead fence with a proclivity for moving stolen goods. Instead, Gerrard was closer to a grandfather-like figure complete with silver beard and a middle-aged paunch that mirrored Morton's own. He had a baby in his arms which he bounced as he looked down at them on the porch.

'Mr Pairac Gerrard?'

'Tá,' Gerrard said. 'Who's askin'?'

'Detective Chief Inspector Morton, Metropolitan Police. This is Inspector Duffy.'

He stepped back to allow them in. 'Then ya'd best come in then before ya freeze ta death. Lemme go hand this one off ta her granny.' Gerrard turned away and called over his shoulder: 'Grab a seat in the front room. Anywhere but the rocker: it's banjaxed.'

They made their way in to find themselves in a lounge that hadn't been redecorated since the eighties. Horrific patterned carpet clashed with peeling wallpaper and the whole room was dominated by an enormous L-shaped sofa which was upholstered in a fuzzy blue-and-pink stripe. Morton made his way over, being careful to dodge the assault course of Lego bricks on the floor.

'This is what ya call a criminal's house?' Aoife whispered. 'Ya sure we're in the right place?'

Before Morton could bite back, Gerrard reappeared without the kid. He perched on the edge of the broken rocking chair.

'Her granny's getting fluthered already so you'd best be quick about you before I got to take 'er back. What is it you're at my door for on Christmas? I'm guessing you're looking to stitch me up fer something. I'd best warn ya I've been out of the game for donkey's years.'

'I find that hard to believe,' Morton said. 'Sixty-two years of life and you've suddenly gone straight in the last four?'

'People change,' Gerrard said. 'I made a complete bags of it all, over and over. When I got out four years ago, I inherited this place from me ole ma. Later that year, my first garinion was born. Sad as it sounds, I changed. I'm too old fer the clink. It's feckin' miserable in there.'

'Then you won't mind us checking out your store for stolen goods.'

'Course not,' Gerrard said. 'Come by any time. We're normally open nine to six, Monday to Saturday. But as you two'll appreciate, it's Christmas so you can bog off 'til after St Stephen's Day unless you've got a warrant?'

He looked from one to the other as if expecting them to produce a court document. 'Thought not.'

'Mr Gerrard,' Aoife said. 'I'll be blunt with ya. We don't give a rat's arse if you're clean or not. Chief Inspector Morton's homicide, I'm with the Anti-Kidnap and Extortion Unit so–'

Gerrard whistled. 'Well, well, well. Never the day I thought I'd have gardai askin' for my help. Let me enjoy this fer a moment... okay, what do you think I can do fer ye?'

'Jewellery,' Aoife said. 'A large quantity of it was stolen from a major department store.'

'Crofte's?'

'How'd you know that?' Morton said.

'Had a fella in the shop last month with loads of stuff, all of it in Crofte's packaging. He wanted a cash price fer it. He was pretty desperate to be honest with you – thought he might be on summat.'

Morton looked at him intently. 'What sort of stuff?'

'Gold but cheap,' Gerrard said. 'The stuff poor people think is expensive. All of it fit for the scrapyard. I told him as much.'

'What'd he say?'

'Asked me to buy it. I told him to sling his hook.'

Morton and Aoife exchanged a disbelieving glance. 'Just like that?'

'Just like that,' Gerrard said. 'I thought he was dodgy. And if he wasn't, it'd have been one of you lot undercover knowing my luck. That's how you got me the last time. Once bitten, twice shy and all that.'

'Do you know where he went?'

'Probably worked his way along the strip.'

'The strip?' Aoife echoed.

'Sorry, it's what we call the row o' pawnbrokers in Kilburn. T' whole place reeks o' desperation. But it's easy money for me and ain't nobody gonna give me a job with my CV.'

'Never tempted to make a few quid on the side?' Morton said.

'Never,' Gerrard said. 'It's just not worth it. Besides, have you seen the paperwork you have to do to keep a scrap metal licence? You can't buy for cash anymore. You've got to keep records, actual, detailed, records of everything you buy. That includes identifying marks on the metal, the name and address of the buyer, even the registration plate of the car they arrive in. Not that they'd let an old lag like me have a licence. But nobody on the strip is dodgy that way. Doing a nixer or handling stolen goods? Sure, some around here'll turn a blind eye – not me before you ask, try Marty's Pawnbrokers across the road from my shop – but never scrap metal. Five grand fines for non-compliance plus the usual criminal penalties for handling stolen goods... you'd have to be a fool to get involved given the margins.'

'You speak as if it's a legitimate business.'

'For fences, it is their business,' Gerrard said, 'and they're fiercely protective of it. Nobody risks jail time for low rewards around here. Not with a London retail presence. You any idea how much we pay in rent and business rates?'

'Then who might?'

Gerrard shrugged. 'Damned if I know. Someone in the Syndicate?'

This was going nowhere. Morton glanced at his watch. It was nearly three. Only two hours until the ransom drop. 'Mr Gerrard, for our records, where were you at three thirty this morning?'

'Asleep. In my bed.'

'Can anyone confirm that?'

'My wife was with me all night though she was asleep too no doubt,' Gerrard said. 'Want me to shout her?'

'That won't be necessary.'

Gerrard stood. 'Then, unless you're arresting me, can we wrap this up? No time like the present, it's Christmas after all. Oh, and detectives, if you did want to bust Marty for handling stolen goods, I hear he's got a safe in his car boot. Just saying.'

Out of the corner of Morton's eye, he saw Aoife crack a thin-lipped smile. They allowed themselves to be ushered out into the cold where Morton stopped on the driveway.

'That was what made you smile? Can we wrap this up? Really? What did you make of Gerrard?'

Aoife looked at him blankly. 'He's as bent as a six bob note but you'll never catch him red-handed. If he's the fence, we're out of luck. What's our next move?'

'The only move we've got left: we go to the drop site and see what happens.'

'Told you–'

'Don't say it,' Morton warned her, wagging a finger.

'So.'

Chapter 14: The Drop

The last two hours flew by in a whirlwind of preparation. There wasn't the budget for air support or a tac unit and so it was on Morton, Aoife and Rafferty to get Kaylee home safe and sound.

The two women had gone ahead to position themselves near the drop site while Morton, as the only man and thus the only one that the kidnappers might plausibly mistake for Leon, was driving Leon's beat up old Ford Focus which was parked around the corner. He wondered once again if he'd have been better off releasing Leon. In the end he couldn't risk it. If Morton did turn out to be wrong and Leon was the mastermind behind this charade then that would be a mistake that Morton could never come back from. Instead Leon was handcuffed to a uniformed officer who had him in the back of a patrol car which by now would be idling in Golder's Green. If Kaylee were safely returned, Leon could be released and reunited with her in time to get home for Christmas.

After he pulled off on Hall Road in St John's Wood, halfway between Crofte's and the drop location in Granville Road, Morton thumbed his police radio. 'Okay, ladies, let's run through the plan one more time. I'm ten minutes out and I'm aiming to arrive dead on five o'clock.'

Rafferty's voice came back straight away with only a trace of radio crackle. 'We're in position. I'm just not north of the derelict house, Aoife's just south. There's no way any suspect is getting in or out without being seen.'

'Good. And the house itself?'

This time Aoife replied. 'I've driven around it. Both the houses on either side are occupied and I've stuck a padlock on the back gate in case our kidnapper tries to leg it on foot.'

'You carry a padlock with you?'

'In my car not my purse. You'd be surprised how much a Belfast lass keeps in her boot.'

Morton set the radio on his dashboard before muttering. 'I don't want to know.'

'Shout when you're in-bound, boss,' Rafferty said.

He waited until twelve minutes to the hour, his pulse racing as the clock ticked down. When it was time, he turned the keys in the ignition. The engine sputtered to life. For a moment, he thought that Leon's car was going to give up the ghost at just the wrong moment. Potential crisis averted, he pulled out into the road and headed east towards Abbey Road. Traffic was exceedingly light and before he knew it, he was racing along the Finchley Road towards the drop zone. He lightened up the pressure on the accelerator to kill a minute or two and cruised north keeping his eyes peeled for any sign of a kidnapper.

Besides him, Leon's burner phone lay on the passenger seat. The battery was fully charged just in case.

As he approached Granville Road, his own phone rang. Brodie. He answered.

'This better be important,' Morton growled.

'The mobile that texted Leon's has just become active. It's connected to a tower near Child's Hill about a hundred and fifty yards south of the drop point.'

'Thanks Brodie. Call Rafferty if you can get us a more precise location.' Morton hung up, grabbed the radio, and told the girls.

The kidnapper was in the vicinity. Or their phone was at least. More importantly, *it wasn't Leon*. He was innocent. Aoife was going to be gutted when she found out.

The goods that Morton and Leon had borrowed from Crofte's were still in the boot, much to the chagrin of Bonaparte.

As he pulled into Granville Road, he grabbed the radio, relayed his position to the girls and tossed it in the passenger-side footwell out of sight and then slunk down low in the driver's seat in case he was being watched. The clock read two minutes to the hour. Now that the sun had set, it was nigh-on impossible to work out which house was right. In the distance, on Morton's left, he could see two houses lit with Christmas lights and a dark void between them. That had to be it. He slowed to a crawl, his eyes darting around the darkness for the slightest sign of movement. Nothing. It was as quiet as a mouse.

He pulled in and killed the engine. His ears pricked for the slightest sound but all he could hear was the sound of his own breath. It was go time.

Morton pocketed the radio from the floor, opened the driver-side door and then stepped out into the night. The darkness which had been such a hindrance was now on his side. The target house was unlit. A broken streetlight meant that only the palest slither of light from the Christmas decorations belonging to the houses on either side lit his way. He unlocked the boot and began to decant its contents onto the pavement. In all, he and Leon had stolen six large carrier bags full of goods. Whether or not it would amount to a hundred thousand pounds' worth remained to be seen. There was scant little information to go on. Would Kaylee be released first? Would one of Tiny's men be standing in the dark waiting to count the lucre? Something was off. Aoife had said the same though her explanation that it was clearly all Leon was now in tatters in light of Brodie's evidence that the kidnapper's phone was active once again.

He approached the gate, set down the three bags in his right hand so that he could open it, and then descended the steep outside staircase which led to a basement-level entrance. According to Leon, the goods had to be left outside the basement entrance. He'd have to make two trips. On the way back up, he felt his feet slip on the ice. His hand shot out to one side, snatching at an old iron handrail. One more careful trip later and all six bags were in the required position outside the basement door.

Now what?

Morton squinted into the darkness. He couldn't see a damned thing.

He opened a radio channel to Rafferty and Aoife. 'Anything?' he whispered.

'Nothing.'

'Nor me.'

This wasn't in the plan.

'Something's off,' Morton said. 'Do you trust me?'

'Of course,' Rafferty's voice came back.

'Absolutely not,' Aoife said. 'Morton, what're ya doing?'

He set the channel to broadcast so that Rafferty and Aoife could hear everything that he could hear and then he clipped his radio to his belt. One deep breath later, he stepped up to the basement door and rapped his fist against it as loudly as he could.

'Police!' he yelled. 'Open up!'

Movement. For the first time he could hear someone moving within.

'Ash, Aoife, watch the ground level, back and front,' Morton yelled. 'Someone's in there.'

He cursed not having a door ram or better backup. Christmas Eve was a brilliant time to commit a crime: half the force was sozzled or celebrating and the other half was stretched so thin that anything short of a shooting-in-progress could wait until Boxing Day.

There was only one thing for it. He had to kick the door in. He turned away from it, leant forward, and then, after a deep breath, mule-kicked the door. His heel struck the lock making the whole door shake within its frame.

'Again,' he muttered. He pulled back and pushed all the way down his core, throwing his weight through his heel and into the door. It gave way.

Inside was pitch black. If someone was in there, he had no way to know where. Presumably, however, any would-be assailant's eyes had already adjusted to the darkness.

'Police!'

'Help!' a voice called out from within. 'Help!'

Almost instinctively Morton headed towards the sound of the voice. A tiny part of him wondered if it were a trap. He reached into his pocket and pulled out his phone and then quickly flipped on the torch. He spun on his heel, scanning the darkness, his muscles tensed as he sought out the voice that had cried out.

There! Out of the corner of his eye, he saw movement. He spun towards the figure, his arm pulling back as his hand balled into a fist.

'Don't hit me!'

It was a woman. 'Kaylee?'

She nodded.

'Where'd he go?'

Dazzled by the light of his torch, she stared at him blankly for a moment and then jerked her head towards the ceiling. Morton grabbed his radio. 'She's safe!. Kidnapper has fled on foot.'

He unstuck the push to talk button so he could hear them if he needed to. Aoife's voice came back strong.

'The building's well covered. I'm calling for back-up. Stay with her, Morton.'

He felt relief flood through him. 'Roger that.'

***

Rafferty sprang into action at Morton's words. 'I'm going in the front at the ground level.'

Much like Morton, she kicked in the front door. It gave way easily illuminating the outline of a person at the end of the hallway.

'It's me!' Aoife said. 'I came in the back. He's not come out this way. I padlocked it earlier and the padlocks back on there now. If he tries to go that way, we'll hear him.'

'Must have gone up then,' Rafferty said. She was closer than Aoife to the stairs and so managed to climb them first, the Irishwoman following a few feet behind. Her heart was pounding. Kaylee might be safe but now the kidnapper was cornered. At the top of the stairs, the hallway split in two.

'You take that way, I'll take this one,' Rafferty whispered. Her side stretched away from Granville Road and towards the back garden.

There were two rooms to clear. When Rafferty reached the first door, she kicked it in without warning.

'Bathroom,' she muttered. Inside was decrepit. Cobwebs crisscrossed back and forth. Nobody had been in here for a long time.

One more room. As she approached the back of the house, the floorboards underneath her creaked to announce her arrival. She swore.

The time for subtlety was gone. Taking a leaf out of Morton's playbook, she announced herself as she approached the last room.

'Police! Come out with your hands up!'

She held her breath, straining for any sounds within. Then, as before, she kicked the door. It swung inwards with such a force that it clattered against the wall behind it and promptly fell off its hinges. Again, cobwebs and dust dominated the room. Nobody had been here in forever and a day. Just in case, Rafferty ducked inside, flashed her torch in every corner, and checked that nobody had fled out the back.

'Aoife!' She yelled. 'Clear back here!'

'Clear,' Aoife echoed.

Rafferty backtracked to the landing to find Aoife waiting for her.

'Attic?' Aoife suggested.

It was the last place to look. Above them was a small square hatch. It too looked unused. Nevertheless, Rafferty interlocked her fingers and cradled her hands. 'Want a boost? Can't see you lifting me.'

Aoife almost smiled. She put one foot in Rafferty's hands and then pushed as she strained to reach the ceiling hatch. With one hand she dislodged it causing years of dust to cascade down upon both of them. They sputtered and choked as they fought to breathe through the ensuing dust cloud.

'Nobody's up there,' Aoife said.

'How the hell did he get by us?' Rafferty asked.

'Nobody could have. Nobody. You'd have to be the invisible man.'

Chapter 15: Backwards

The girls emerged from the house apologetic and ashamed. Despite their best efforts, the kidnapper had got away. Morton reassured Aoife and Rafferty that there was nothing more they could have done and then turned his attention to Kaylee.

She was sitting in the warmth of Rafferty's car, a silver thermal blanket laid over her back and Morton keeping her company. An ambulance had been called, not that Kaylee seemed to need one. She wasn't exhibiting any signs of shock. Nor had she been bound.

She looked at Morton with big brown eyes, her smudged mascara making her look like a panda. 'He held a gun on me.'

'All day?' Morton asked.

'Enough that I knew it was there. I didn't dare move.'

Morton shifted in his seat so he could twist round and look at her properly. 'Run me through it all again. This all started when?'

'Early,' Kaylee said. 'I heard Leon leave. He always slams the door, bless him. Then I heard a knock. I thought the daft git had forgotten his keys again.'

'How long was there between the slam and the knock?'

'Dunno, I was half asleep. Not long.'

'Then what happened?'

'I opened the door and a man in a balaclava pointed a gun in my face, told me to come with him and not to say a word. He stood back and made me walk in front of him along the corridor and down the stairs. When we got outside, he marched me to his van. At that point, he blindfolded me, tied my hands behind my back and shoved me in the van.'

He glanced down at her wrists. In the darkness, they didn't look marked or abraded. He ignored that and instead asked: 'Did he drive you somewhere?'

'Yeah, some dodgy garage. I don't know where.'

'A mechanics?'

'I guess.'

Morton's suspicions grew. 'What do you mean you guess? Was it a mechanics? Or a large residential garage?'

'Err... the latter. I could smell oil and rubber.'

'Okay. Was anyone else there?'

'No. Just him. He kept the balaclava on all day.'

'Right,' Morton said. 'You were in this large residential garage that you said was "dodgy". How was it dodgy?'

'It just felt like it was like really downmarket?'

Downmarket? Morton thought. *Downmarket?!* She was from Kilburn. How much more downmarket could you get? Upper Norwood?

'And like, the seats were like totally worn out.'

'What seats were there?'

'Umm, sofas. Two of them. And a low table. He sat on one sofa and I sat on the other. At lunchtime he gave me a can of cola and a bag of salt and vinegar crisps.'

'Did you do anything? Did he speak at all?'

Kaylee paused. 'I went to the loo.'

'How did that work?'

She looked puzzled. 'Like... regular pee?'

'I meant,' Morton said with more patience than he felt, 'did he come in with you? Or did he wait outside? Was there a window or a vent in the bathroom?'

'No window,' Kaylee said. 'He waited outside. He told me to hurry up a couple of times.'

'And this was before lunch?'

'Uhuh.'

'What sort of voice did he have?'

'Manly,' she said firmly. 'Very deep. Gruff. Probably Eastern European?'

'Right. What did you do all day?'

'We sat.'

'Weren't you scared?'

'I was... but if he wanted me dead, why did he keep me there?'

'Did he keep your hands tied?' Morton asked. 'I only ask because your wrists don't seem to be marked at all.'

'It was like silk. He tied them with silk.'

'How very considerate,' Morton said. 'And this gentleman kidnapper, did he say anything?'

'Not until we got here. Then all he said was "It's time."'

'Very ominous. What did you think that meant?'

'I had no idea. I was just scared. I wasn't thinking at all.'

Morton leant back. 'Just to double check, you're telling me it went like this: Leon left, door knocked, gun pulled, frogmarched, blindfolded then tied, back of the van, garage, sofa, loo, crisps and diet cola, back in the van, here, talking to me.'

'Yep,' Kaylee said, flashing a smile. 'That was when you rescued me.'

'And he ran upstairs?'

'Err...Like, I think so. Yeah, he must have done.'

'Because there aren't any stairs between the basement and the main house. They're totally separate dwellings.'

'Oh no, I meant he said he was upstairs. Would be upstairs. While I was to wait downstairs.'
It didn't add up at all. 'He told you to wait... so you did?'
'He had a gun!'
'Okay,' Morton said. 'Tell me it all again. In reverse this time.'
'Huh? Why?'
Morton smiled sweetly back at her. 'Humour me.'
'Okay. You rescued me and before that I was in the dark. Before that he was upstairs-'
'He was upstairs?' Morton interjected.
'I mean, we were upstairs. Coming down. Outside. Before that we were in the van. Then I peed, had a diet coke, lunch... err... tied hands... in the van... no, wait, tied hands, gun, frog-marched...'
'Can't keep it straight in your head, can you Kaylee?' Morton asked. 'It's a classic sign of a lie. Liars rehearse their lies over and over but only in a linear fashion. You did okay when you were telling me your made-up story the first time but you can't tell me it in reverse, can you? You swapped the bathroom visit around, had your hands tied after you got in the van rather than before, and couldn't work out where he was while you were downstairs.'
She looked at him as if butter wouldn't melt in her mouth. 'That doesn't prove anything. I could have made an honest mistake.'
It wasn't a denial.
'True,' Morton said, still smiling. 'But I'm sure that now I know you're a liar, I can find plenty of evidence. But let's start with the basics. What do you do for a living?'
'I'm an accountant.'
'No, you're not. There isn't a single mention of you on Google and the firm you claim to work for? They've never heard of you. Let's try it again: where do you work?'

'I don't, okay?' Kaylee said. 'Is that a crime now?'

'Lying to the police is. Where do you go all day? Leon said you've been leaving at half seven every day for years and not coming home before eight o'clock in the evening. That's a long time to wander the streets doing nothing.'

She mumbled something he couldn't quite hear.

'Sorry?'

She mumbled again, louder this time. 'I want a deal.'

'The only deal I can offer you is this: come clean, tell me everything, and I'll tell the court you co-operated. If you don't, I'll make sure Kieran O'Connor at the CPS throws the book at you.'

'Fine,' she said. All the pretence of sweetness and light disappeared along with her smile. 'I don't have a job. I've never had one. I don't have a single qualification beyond my O-Levels, okay? When that feckless husband of mine got fired, he thought I would take up the slack. He ruined me. Our friends – police detectives, their wives and families – shunned us overnight. We had it all and then we had nothing.'

'Sounds tough,' Morton said. 'What did you do?'

'I tried to find work. I really did. I took hundreds of copies of my CV and went out walking the streets, stopping in every office and shop I saw. That's what my father told me to do. It didn't work. Nobody wants a paper CV anymore. It's all online application this and e-interview that. Nobody wanted a woman with no qualifications and no experience.'

'So you had to find another way to pay the bills. It's been you blackmailing Leon the entire time.'

'The great bogeyman,' Kaylee said. 'Leon cared more about Tiny Bakowski and what he was doing than he ever cared about my wants or needs. I'm not ashamed to say I used it. Crofte's makes millions of pounds a week and they pay him ten pounds an hour. You can't feed a dog for that money.'

'You helped yourself.'

'I did,' Kaylee said, shrugging. 'They didn't miss the money and we needed it.'

'Until August.'

'Until November.'

'Nope, Leon was ahead of you. He stole enough that he kept several months in hand at a time...'

Her eyes lit up. 'That's my Leon.'

'And then in November, he finally ran out. Presumably that's when you concocted this plan?'

'Yep,' she said. 'It's Christmas. Everyone is spending money on plastic tat and designer rags. Why shouldn't we get a taste?'

'Speaking of that, where has the money gone? You've stolen ten thousand a month every month for years... but you live in a rat-infested dump in Kilburn.'

'I couldn't just flash the cash. Everyone knew Leon was dirty. It was all over the papers. I had to play it cool at first, I just spent the money on experiences. Nice spas, trips abroad – I told Leon I was travelling for business – and then...'

'Then what?'

'I met someone.'

'A man?'

'A man,' Kaylee said. 'A wonderful, kind man. His name was Paraic-'

'Gerrard,' Morton finished for her. He knew the scumbag had been lying.

'How did you know?'

'More importantly,' Morton countered, 'how did you meet?'

'I was flogging the jewellery that Leon stole. Paraic has been a god-send in turning that tat into ready cash. And he's nice.'

'Hasn't he got a wife?'

'She's dead. Lung cancer, years ago.'

'I heard her earlier...'

'You heard me earlier,' Kaylee corrected. 'I was at Paraic's the whole time. He handed me the baby and then fobbed you off.'

'Your baby?'

'His grandbaby. I can't have kids...'

'And Paraic came with a built-in family,' Morton surmised. 'He was missing a mother and a wife, not to mention cash and a career, and along you came to fill those voids.'

'I gave him everything. I raised his kids. I took him on holidays. And yet...'

'And yet you were still irrevocably tied to Leon. Without him, the cash cow ended.'

'Today was going to be the last time,' Kaylee said. 'A hundred grand. Enough to get us out. I was going to disappear. Well, Kaylee Yap was. She was going to die and Paraic was getting me new papers, perfect fakes, so that I could be his wife, his partner, all the time.'

'It almost worked too,' Kaylee said. 'I never thought he'd ask you for help.'

'And yet he did,' Morton said. He produced his handcuffs. 'Kaylee Yap, you're under arrest for extortion.'

He gave her the full caution, snapped his cuffs on her wrists, and stepped out of the car. While he had been interviewing her, the ambulance had arrived and so had the police car that Leon was in.

Leon ran towards the Saab as soon as he almost immediately. He saw his wife in the back of the Saab and immediately put two and two together. Morton leapt out to intercept him, throwing out his right arm to stop Leon getting any closer.

It was then that he broke, sinking to his knees and wailing in the most pitiful way.

'Leon, I'm sorry.'

'Me too. I thought you'd finally get that bastard Bakowski – for the both of us. Are you going to arrest me now too?'

Could he arrest a man who'd lost everything: his career, his wife, his dignity? And on Christmas?

The twinkling of Christmas lights on a house in the distance drew Morton's gaze. Whether or not someone believed in Christmas, there was never any harm in being kind.

'Stand up, Leon,' Morton said. 'And start walking towards my car.'

He stood. 'Am I under arrest?'

Morton cracked a smile. 'Nope... You're coming to mine for Christmas tea. It might have to be reheated though. Sarah said the boys ate without me hours ago. But first, we've got swing by Crofte's to return all the stuff we borrowed.'

Sometime, Christmas could be murder. But not this Christmas.

From the Author

Thanks for reading Christmas Can Be Murder. I had a blast writing it and hope you loved it just as much. If you'd like to check out other books I've written, you can find them all at DCIMorton.com or by searching for Sean Campbell on your local Amazon store. This is the official series reading order (which you can ignore if you like – the stories can be read in any order):

DCI Morton:

1. Dead on Demand
2. Cleaver Square
3. Ten Guilty Men
4. The Patient Killer
5. The Evolution of a Serial Killer
6. Double Blind

DI Rafferty featuring DCI Morton:

1. Missing Persons

Merry Christmas!
Sean

Printed in Great Britain
by Amazon